Elspeth Rawstron 著

李璞良 譯

The Kingdom of the Snow Leopard

雪豹王國

CONTENTS

Hello Elspeth, tell us a little about yourself.

I studied drama at university and then worked for a theater newspaper in London. Later, I decided to train as an English teacher and work in Italy, my favorite country. By a strange twist[1] of fate, I got a teaching job in Istanbul in Turkey and I have lived and worked there teaching and writing ever since.

How are you inspired to write your stories?

Story ideas can come from a casual conversation, a visit to a new city or country, an article in a magazine or newspaper or, as in this case, the Internet.

Elspeth Rawstron

How did you think of this story?

One day my friend, Halime, was surfing the Net for information about countries around the world. She was fascinated[2] by a site about a Tibetan Buddhist kingdom in the Himalayas and she showed it to me. The kingdom was Bhutan, the Kingdom of the Thunder Dragon, and when I read about it, I was inspired to write this story.

One thing that struck me when I was reading the article were the King's words: "Gross national happiness is more important than gross national product[3]." Happiness is more important than wealth. Those words stayed with me and inspired me to write this story.

I was also inspired by the fact that Bhutan was isolated[4] and unaffected by the outside world for centuries. The idea formed to write about a country where there are no cars, no TV, no Coca-Cola, no McDonald's or globalization[5]. Of course, the Kingdom of the Snow Leopard is a fictional place and all the characters in it are fictional.

I hope that you will enjoy this story and will be inspired to learn about different cultures and travel to far-off magical places where all kinds of adventures can happen.

---

1 twist [twɪst] (n.) 轉折
2 fascinated [ˋfæsṇˏetɪd] (a.) 著迷的
3 gross national product 國民生產總值（GNP）
4 isolated [ˋaɪsḷˏetɪd] (a.) 孤立的
5 globalization [ˏglobəlaɪˋzeʃən] (n.) 全球化

1 The title of the story is *The Kingdom of the Snow Leopard* and there is a legend about a snow leopard in the story. Read and listen to the information about snow leopards.

The Snow Leopard

Snow leopards live in Central Asia and the Himalayan Mountains of Bhutan, India, Nepal and Tibet. They are endangered animals and there are less than 10,000 of them alive today.

2 Listen to Sarah Williams from the WWF talking about snow leopards. Then answer the questions below.

- a Where can you find snow leopards?
- b How long is an adult male snow leopard?
- c Why do they need long tails?
- d Why have they got wide noses?
- e How do they balance on top of the snow?
- f What do they eat?
- g How far can a snow leopard jump?
- h How much does a baby snow leopard weigh?

2 Tigers are also mentioned in the story. Do some research about tigers on the Internet and write a short paragraph about them.

3 Look quickly at the pictures in the book and answer the questions.

a Where do you think the story takes place? Tick 2 continents.
☐ America ☐ Asia ☐ Africa ☐ Europe ☐ Australia

b What kind of story is it? Tick.
☐ Thriller ☐ Adventure ☐ Detective Story ☐ Romance

4 Look at the pictures below. Discuss.

① Which picture do you prefer? Give reasons.
② Which place would you like to visit? Give reasons.

5 Now write short descriptions of the places mentioned above. What do you think the two places are and where are they?

6 Match the words from the story with the pictures.

_____ a cave   _____ e gun
_____ b throne   _____ f bow
_____ c mask   _____ g arrow
_____ d temple   _____ h monks

7 The words are all important to the story. Can you guess how?
Use each of the words above to complete the sentences.

(a) The room was full of .... in orange robes
who were chanting.

(b) The King sat down on his ....

(c) The man was holding a .... to her head.

(d) The .... whizzed through the air towards
the target.

(e) After climbing for an hour they came to a small
....

(f) The man pulled off the golden dragon ....
and laughed.

(g) He was carrying a mediaeval-style helmet and his
....

(h) When we walked into the Buddhist ....,
there was silence.

8 Choose one of the sentences. Continue the story from there.

The two boys sat on a bench under a big old oak tree. There was a lawn[1] in front of them and, in front of that, the huge[2] iron gates of the school. The two boys often came and sat here after lessons.

Tom was tall with fair hair and blue eyes. His friend, Mahir, had black hair and dark brown eyes.

Tom was excited and Mahir was smiling.

"Are you sure you want me to come?" asked Tom.

"Yes, of course. I've told you so much about my kingdom. Now I want you to see it for yourself[2]," replied Mahir.

"Fantastic[3]," said Tom. "I'd love to come. I'll have to ask my mum and dad, of course. But I'm sure they'll be fine about it."

"Tom," said Mahir. His voice was serious now. "You've been a really good friend. You stood up for[4] me when the others picked on[5] me. They made fun of my accent[6] and appearance[7]. But you didn't. I hated this school at the beginning and I hated this country and all the people in it. But your friendship changed everything. And I'll always appreciate[8] that. Thanks."

"There's no need to thank me, Mahir. I was on my own[9] too. And you were fun, and interesting."

"Thanks, anyway. I'm really happy here now."

"Good," said Tom. "Now, let's talk about more important things."

"Such as . . .?"

---

1 lawn [lɔn] (n.) 草坪；草地
2 see it for yourself 親自去看看
3 fantastic [fænˋtæstɪk] (a.) 〔口〕
　太好了
4 stand up for sb 維護某人

5 pick on sb 找某人的碴
6 accent [ˋæksɛnt] (n.) 口音；腔調
7 appearance [əˋpɪrəns] (n.) 外貌
8 appreciate [əˋpriʃɪˏet] (v.) 感激
9 on my own 自己一個人

"My visit to the coolest country in the world," said Tom. "Do I need a visa[1] to go there?"

"Yes, you do. All foreigners need a visa. Only 5,000 tourists[2] are allowed to come every year. My father, the King doesn't want our country to lose its culture[3]. He is afraid that tourists will change the country," said Mahir.

"So it's no Coca-Cola and no McDonald's for a month, then," said Tom.

"Correct," said Mahir and he laughed. "Do you think you can live without them?"

"I think I can—but can you?" laughed Tom.

Suddenly Tom saw a tiny[4] flash[5] of light. "Hey, what was that?"

"It looked like a camera flash," said Mahir.

"I think there's someone down there by the gate!" said Tom and he stood up quickly.

There was another flash. Mahir and Tom ran towards the gate. Tom was sure it was a camera. "Who are you?" he shouted. "What are the photographs for?"

The man didn't answer. He turned and ran away. He was tall and thin. He was bald[6] and had brown eyes. His face was not very memorable[7] except for the long scar[8] that ran from the corner of his left eye down to the corner of his mouth.

"Why do you think he was taking photographs of you?" asked Tom.

1 visa ['vizə] (n.) 簽證
2 tourist ['tʊrɪst] (n.) 觀光客
3 culture ['kʌltʃə] (n.) 文化
4 tiny ['taɪnɪ] (a.) 微小的
5 flash [flæʃ] (n.) 閃光
6 bald [bɔld] (a.) 禿頭的
7 memorable ['mɛmrəbl] (a.) 顯著的
8 scar [skɑr] (n.) 疤
9 concern [kənˋsɝn] (v.) 擔心
10 bodyguard ['bɑdɪˏgɑrd] (n.) 保鏢
11 scared [skɛrd] (a.) 嚇壞的
12 murderer ['mɝdərə] (n.) 殺手
13 thriller ['θrɪlə] (n.) 驚悚片
14 opponent [əˋponənt] (n.) 對手

"I don't know," said Mahir.

"What if he's dangerous? I think we should tell one of the teachers about him," said Tom.

"No, I don't want to do that," said Mahir quickly.

"Well, I think you should tell your father then," said Tom, concerned[9].

"No, he'll only worry about me and then he'll send me more bodyguards[10]. I don't want that," said Mahir.

"But aren't you scared[11]? That man might be a murderer[12]! He might try to kill you," said Tom.

"Oh yeah! I think you've seen too many thrillers[13]," said Mahir.

"I can look after myself. You know that, Tom."

Then Mahir took Tom's arm and with one quick move, he threw him over his back to the ground.

"Okay, okay, I know," said Tom. "You can look after yourself. That throw was perfect. It didn't hurt at all."

"You should never hurt your opponent[14]. You should only block[15] him," said Mahir. "Those are the rules of combat[16] in my country. Now, stand up."

"You know, I can't," said Tom.

He couldn't move his arms or legs. They felt very heavy. He couldn't even move a finger. It was amazing[17]! Mahir walked slowly over to Tom. He laid his hand on his shoulder and pressed[18] with his thumb. "Now, get up," he said calmly. And Tom got up.

"How do you do it?" asked Tom.

"I practice ," said Mahir. "Remember, 'practice makes perfect.' Now you try."

15 block [blɑk] (v.) 阻止
16 combat [ˋkɑmbæt] (n.) 格鬥
17 amazing [əˋmezɪŋ] (a.) 驚人的
18 press [prɛs] (v.) 按壓

Strength

- Have you ever done a martial art? What do you know about the following martial arts? What skills do they develop?

  (a) Judo[1]   (b) Karate[2]   (c) Aikido[3]

  (d) Tai Chi[4]   (e) Kickboxing[5]   (f) Kung Fu

Tom took Mahir's arm and pressed with his fingers. Then he threw him over his back onto the ground. Mahir stood up immediately. "The throw was good," he said. "But you need to work on your powers of concentration[6]."

"I'll never be able to do it," said Tom.

"You will," said Mahir calmly. "You're definitely[7] improving[8]. If you believe you can do it, you will do it. And now I think it's time for dinner. Let's go!"

"Okay, I'm starving[9]. Race you to the canteen[10]!"said Tom.

Of course, Mahir won. He always won at sports. He was very fit[11] and strong. Tom thought back to their first week at school together. They were both eleven and they were both very homesick. Life at the expensive boarding school[12] in the south of England was very difficult. One night, they couldn't sleep. It was a warm night in early September. So they crept[13] out of the dormitory[14] together and went outside into the school grounds. They walked down the long driveway[15] and sat under the oak tree on the wooden bench. This was to be the beginning of a long friendship.

That night, Mahir told Tom a story—a story that Tom will never forget. It was the story of the secret to Mahir's strength.

"When I was four, my father, the King, took me to a Buddhist[16] monastery[17] high up in the Himalayan Mountains. There were no roads to the monastery. There were only small paths up the mountains. It was snowing very heavily and the ground was icy. The journey was very difficult. My father left me at the monastery with an old monk. When we first walked into the monastery, I was very frightened. The monks were chanting[18] loudly, the air was thick with smoke from the incense[19] and there was a strange sweet smell. I held my father's hand tightly and hid my face in his robe[20]. Then the old monk walked down a long red carpet towards me. He was smiling and he had kind eyes. When he reached me, he took my hand and held it. It was a freezing[21] cold day but I felt warm and I didn't feel frightened any more. And I have never been frightened since that day. I stayed with the monk for seven years. He taught me many things. He taught me to control my mind. He taught me to conquer[22] fear. He taught me to survive[23] without food. He taught me to stay warm in freezing cold temperatures[24]. And he taught me to fight and win but not hurt anybody."

1 judo ['dʒudo] (n.) 柔道
2 karate [kə'rɑtɪ] (n.) 空手道
3 aikido [aɪ'kido] (n.) 合氣道
4 tai chi [taɪ dʒi] (n.) 太極拳
5 kickboxing ['kɪk,bɑksɪŋ] (n.) 跆拳道
6 concentration [,kɑnsɛn'treʃən] (n.) 專注
7 definitely ['dɛfənɪtlɪ] (adv.) 明顯地
8 improve [ɪm'pruv] (v.) 進步
9 starving ['stɑrvɪŋ] (a.) 極飢餓的
10 canteen [kæn'tin] (n.) 學校的餐廳
11 fit [fɪt] (a.) 強健的
12 boarding school 寄宿學校
13 creep [krip] (v.) 躡手躡足地走（動詞三態：creep; crept/creeped; crept/creeped）
14 dormitory ['dɔrmə,torɪ] (n.) 學生宿舍
15 driveway ['draɪv,we] (n.) 汽車道
16 Buddhist ['bʊdɪst] (a.) 佛教的
17 monastery ['mɑnəs,tɛrɪ] (n.) 僧院
18 chant [tʃænt] (v.) 唱誦
19 incense ['ɪnsɛns] (n.) 香
20 robe [rob] (n.) 長袍
21 freezing ['frizɪŋ] (a.) 極冷的
22 conquer ['kɑŋkɚ] (v.) 戰勝
23 survive [sɚ'vaɪv] (v.) 活下來
24 temperature ['tɛmprətʃɚ] (n.) 溫度

INDEPENDENCE

- When was the first time you stayed away from home? How long did you stay away for? Who did you stay with?
- If you were sent away to a monastery for a year, what would you miss from home? Make a list. Share with a partner.

"Will you teach me?" Tom had asked.

Mahir looked at him for a long time. Then he said, "I think we will be friends. And I will teach you."

That was five years ago. Now they were very close friends and Mahir had taught Tom many things.

Finally, it was the last day of term[1]. Tom felt very excited. His mum and dad were coming to collect[2] him and Mahir in an hour. Tom still couldn't believe that he was really going.

He was in the dorm[3]. He was packing[4] his case[5] when Cornelius came and sat on his bed. Tom didn't like Cornelius. He was clever and witty[6], but he was also very mean[7]. He used to[8] tease[9] Mahir a lot in their first year at school. Tom and Mahir avoided him as much as possible.

"I hear you're going to spend the Christmas holidays with Mahir in that weird[10] country of his," said Cornelius. "You must be mad!"

---

1 term [tɝm] (n.) 學期
2 collect [kəˈlɛkt] (v.) 接走
3 dorm [dɔrm] (n.) 學生宿舍
4 pack [pæk] (v.) 打包
5 case [kes] (n.) 箱；盒
6 witty [ˈwɪtɪ] (a.) 詼諧的
7 mean [min] (a.) 卑鄙的
8 used to 以前常常……
9 tease [tiz] (v.) 取笑
10 weird [wɪrd] (a.) 〔口〕奇怪的；神祕的

"It's not a weird country," said Tom angrily. "And I'm really looking forward to[1] going there with Mahir."

"Are you sure you want to go to a country that doesn't have TV or the Internet[2] or a mobile phone[3] network? You'll get bored," said Cornelius.

"There are more important things in life than TV and the Internet," said Tom.

"Like what?" asked Cornelius.

"Like travelling and learning about different cultures. Seeing how other people live."

"Fascinating," said Cornelius and he yawned. "Well I'm going skiing in Switzerland with my parents this Christmas. We're going to stay in a luxury[4] hotel equipped[5] with all the latest technology[6]."

"Well, I hope you enjoy it," said Tom.

"Yes, I will," said Cornelius. "Well, I suppose I'll see you next term but maybe I won't. Maybe they'll keep you prisoner[7] in that weird country. Or maybe you'll be attacked[8] by a yeti[9] and die there."

"Very funny, Cornelius," said Tom. "Now I have to finish packing this case."

Cornelius sat around for a while and then left.

After he had finished packing, Tom went to find Mahir. "Where is he?" he thought. "I haven't seen him all morning. And Mum and Dad will be here soon."

---

1 look forward to 期待（後接名詞或動名詞）
2 Internet [ˈɪntɚˌnɛt] (n.) 網際網路
3 mobile phone [ˈmobɪl fon] 手機
4 luxury [ˈlʌkʃərɪ] (a.) 豪華的
5 equipped with 裝有……設備
6 technology [tɛkˈnɑlədʒɪ] (n.) 科技
7 prisoner [ˈprɪznɚ] (n.) 囚犯
8 attack [əˈtæk] (v.) 攻擊
9 yeti [ˈjɛtɪ] (n.) 傳說中的喜馬拉雅山雪人
10 Tibetan [tɪˈbɛtən] (a.) 藏語的
11 script [skrɪpt] (n.) 筆跡

Mahir was coming to stay at Tom's house for the night. And of course, his bodyguard was coming too. Then the next day, they were going to the airport. They were travelling to the Kingdom of the Snow Leopard together.

Tom had a special invitation from the King. He was very proud of that. It was in his pocket now. It was a white card with something written on it in a beautiful Tibetan[10] script[11] in red and gold.

Tom finally found Mahir. He was sitting on their bench and he was watching all the parents drive into the school grounds. Tom sat on the bench with him and they waited for his mum and dad to arrive. "Thank goodness it's the end of term," thought Tom. "I don't think I could stand one more night in the dorm. I just want to sleep in a room by myself again."

"No more school bells," said Mahir interrupting Tom's thoughts.

"No more cold lumpy[12] porridge[13] for breakfast," said Tom.

"No more French vocabulary tests," said Mahir.

"No more detention[14] with Mr Myers," said Tom.

"And no more running around on a frozen football pitch[15] on Saturday mornings," said Mahir.

"I thought you liked sport," said Tom.

"I do," said Mahir," but not football. I like sports that require concentration or skill like judo or karate or archery[16]."

The two boys continued their game of "No More . . ." until Tom's father's silver car drove through the school gates.

---

12 lumpy [ˈlʌmpɪ] (a.) 有塊狀物的   15 football pitch 足球場
13 porridge [ˈpɔrɪdʒ] (n.) 粥   16 archery [ˈɑrtʃərɪ] (n.) 箭術
14 detention [dɪˈtɛnʃən] (n.) 扣留

The next morning, Mahir dressed in his traditional dress. He wore a gho, a long robe, tied around the waist by a piece of cloth called a kera. The gho was made of beautiful red and gold woven[1] silk and there was a golden dragon with red eyes on each sleeve.

"Now he looks like a real prince," Tom thought.

Tom wasn't taking much with him. He had some presents for the King and Queen and for Mahir's sister and four younger brothers.

"You don't need to take many clothes," Mahir said. "You'll have to wear traditional clothes when you get to the Kingdom."

They were flying[2] with British[3] Airways[4] to Kathmandu[5] in Nepal[6]. Then from there they were catching another plane to the Kingdom of the Snow Leopard. There was only one airline that flew to the Kingdom. It was the country's own airline[7], Dragon Air. And it only flew there twice a week from Kathmandu and once a week from Bangkok.

When they landed in Kathmandu, it was 3 o'clock in the afternoon. Two monks from the palace were there to meet them. They bowed[8]. Then one of them spoke to Mahir and handed him a parcel[9]. Mahir thanked him and then turned to Tom. "These are your clothes," said Mahir. "You should put them on now. Samir will help you."

One of the monks stepped forward and bowed to Tom. Then he led Tom to the executive[10] lounge[11]. There were showers and changing rooms there. Tom opened the parcel and he carefully lifted out the dark blue and gold gho. The monk helped him to wind[12] the cloth around his body and then tie the kera. Tom was taller than most people in the Kingdom of the Snow Leopard, so his clothes had all been specially made for him. The blue of the robe made his eyes look even bluer. When he looked in the mirror, Tom was impressed. "Now I look like a prince, too," he thought. Then he walked out to join Mahir in the VIP[13] lounge.

1 weave [wiv] (v.) 編織（動詞三態：weave; wove/weaved; woven/wove/weaved）
2 fly [flaɪ] (v.) 飛（動詞三態：fly; flew; flown）
3 British [ˋbrɪtɪʃ] (a.) 英國的
4 airways [ˋɛr͵wez] (n.)〔口〕航空公司
5 Kathmandu [͵kætmænˋdu] (n.)（尼泊爾首都）加德滿都
6 Nepal [niˋpɔl] (n.) 尼泊爾
7 airline [ˋɛr͵laɪn] (n.) 飛機航線
8 bow [baʊ] (v.) 鞠躬
9 parcel [ˋpɑrsḷ] (n.) 包裹
10 executive [ɪgˋzɛkjʊtɪv] (a.) 高級享受的
11 lounge [laʊndʒ] (n.) 休息室；候機室
12 wind [waɪnd] (v.) 纏繞（動詞三態：wind; wound; wound）
13 VIP (n.) 重要貴賓（= very important person 重要人物）

While he was walking to the lounge, he saw the man with the scar. His heart began to beat[1] very fast. The man looked away.

"Why is this man here and why is he following Mahir?" Tom asked himself. He watched the man walk into the cafeteria[2]. Then he walked quickly back to the lounge.

"What's the matter?" asked Mahir when he saw the worried look on Tom's face.

"That man with the scar is here in the airport. The man who took photographs of you in the school grounds," said Tom, a note[3] of panic[4] in his voice.

"I know. I saw him in the airport in London too," said Mahir.

"You didn't tell me," said Tom.

"I didn't want to frighten you," said Mahir. "That man is watching me but he can't harm me."

"You don't know that. He could shoot[5] you," said Tom. "He could kill you."

"No, he won't do that," said Mahir calmly[6]. "He didn't kill me in England and he won't kill me here. He wants something from me but I don't know what it is. We have to be patient and wait. We'll find out soon."

"Are you sure?" asked Tom.

"Yes, I am," said Mahir. But Mahir wasn't sure.

"What does the man want?" he asked himself. "Does he want to kill me or does he want to kidnap[7] me? Then why didn't he do it in England? It was easier there. In the palace, there are hundreds of people watching me. The Kingdom of the Snow Leopard is a peaceful country. I hope he won't bring violence[8]."

 14

"Hey, Mahir," said Tom. "They're calling our flight. Come on! Let's get on the plane."

"Let's go," said Mahir and he smiled at his friend. "You're going to love this flight."

It was a very small plane. It only took thirty-five passengers[9]. "Wicked[10]!" said Tom. "I've never been on such a small plane."

"You're lucky this is a daytime flight," said Mahir. "We'll be able to see Mount Everest. You're about to fly past the summit[11] of the highest mountain in the world."

"Cool!" said Tom. "That's better than climbing it any day."

They sat down and fastened[12] their seatbelts. Then Tom looked up and he saw the man with the scar enter the plane.

"I don't believe it," he said. "That man's getting on our plane. He's coming to the Kingdom of the Snow Leopard."

"Don't worry, Tom," said Mahir calmly. "He won't do anything yet."

"But what if he hijacks[13] the plane?" asked Tom.

"No," said Mahir. "He won't do that. I've told you, he wants something from my country. Now let's forget about him and enjoy the flight."

---

1 beat [bit] (v.) 跳動;拍打(動詞三態:beat; beat; beat)
2 cafeteria [ˌkæfəˈtɪrɪə] (n.) 自助餐廳
3 note [not] (n.) 口氣
4 panic [ˈpænɪk] (n.) 恐慌
5 shoot [ʃut] (v.) 射殺(動詞三態:shoot; shot; shot)
6 calmly [ˈkɑmlɪ] (adv.) 平靜地
7 kidnap [ˈkɪdnæp] (v.) 綁架
8 violence [ˈvaɪələns] (n.) 暴力
9 passenger [ˈpæsndʒɚ] (n.) 乘客
10 wicked [ˈwɪkɪd] (a.) 〔俚〕很棒的
11 summit [ˈsʌmɪt] (n.) 峰頂
12 fasten [ˈfæsṇ] (v.) 繫緊
13 hijack [ˈhaɪˌdʒæk] (v.) 劫持

The plane took off[1] and Tom saw the Himalayas in front of them. The plane flew higher and higher until the huge mountain range[2] was below them. Tom held his breath[3] as the plane climbed and climbed. The view of the snowy white peaks[4] below them was spectacular[5].

"We're lucky the weather is fine today. Sometimes it's very windy and the journey can be very frightening," said Mahir.

An hour and a half later, the small plane landed in the Kingdom of the Snow Leopard. Tom was relieved[6].

"We're safe for the moment. The man with the scar didn't hijack the plane," he thought.

"Look," said Mahir and he pointed out of the window. "My mother and father have come to meet us."

Tom looked out of the window. There were people standing outside the small airport building. There were monks in long orange robes and there were men in red and gold robes. In the center, there was a man and a woman. They were sitting on two chairs.

"They must be Mahir's mother and father," thought Tom.

The plane stopped in front of a long red carpet. When the air steward[7] opened the door of the plane, Tom could hear music. It was strange and haunting[8] and it sounded like pipes. They sat and waited until the other passengers had got off the plane.

The monks were giving the passengers little bracelets of orange flowers. "What are they giving the passengers?" asked Tom.

---

1 take off 起飛
2 range [rendʒ] (n.) 山脈
3 hold one's breath 屏息
4 peak [pik] (n.) 山頂
5 spectacular [spɛk`tækjələ] (a.) 壯觀的
6 relieved [rɪ`livd] (a.) 放心的
7 steward [`stjuwəd] (n.) 男服務員
8 haunting [`hɔntɪŋ] (a.) 給人以強烈感受

"That small orange flower is a symbol[1] of happiness. Those people are our guests and we hope that they'll be happy in our country," said Mahir.

Tom watched the man with the scar walk quickly along the red carpet and then disappear into the airport building. "Maybe I should tell Mahir's father about him," thought Tom.

When Tom and Mahir finally walked down the red carpet, the monks bowed in greeting. And they gave Tom and Mahir each a bracelet of orange flowers. The King and Queen now stood at the end of the carpet. Mahir bowed to his father and then to his mother. Tom copied him.

1 symbol [ˈsɪmbl̩] (n.) 象徵
2 formality [fɔrˈmælətɪ] (n.) 禮節
3 carriage [ˈkærɪdʒ] (n.) 馬車
4 set off 動身

"Welcome to the Kingdom of the Snow Leopard," said the King in English.

"Thank you," said Tom. "I'm very happy to be here."

Then the monks walked out through the airport building and the King and Queen followed them. Nobody else's parents greeted Tom in this way. The formality[2] of the greeting made him feel important and he quite liked it.

Outside there was a horse and carriage[3]. The King and Queen got in and Mahir and Tom followed them. Then the carriage set off[4].

The carriage drove along a wide road lined with trees. People waved as they passed by[1], and they threw flowers.

"It's very quiet for a capital[2] city," thought Tom. Then he realized[6] why. There were no cars on the road.

"There aren't any cars here!" he said, surprised.

"No," said the King. "Cars cause pollution[4]. They fill the cities and they bring a lot of stress to people's lives. Here people ride horses or bicycles. They move around the city freely. They don't sit for hours in traffic jams[5]."

"Cool," said Tom. But he couldn't imagine his own father going to work on a bicycle and he definitely couldn't imagine his mother going shopping on a horse.

Suddenly they went round a corner in the road and Tom saw a huge mountain in front of them. There, high up on the slope[6] of the mountain, was a building painted in red, black and gold.

"That's the palace," said Mahir.

"Wow!" said Tom. "It's amazing."

Ten minutes later, the carriage stopped before two huge wooden gates. The palace guards opened the gates and they drove through. Then the gates shut behind them.

"Has anyone ever tried to attack the palace?" asked Tom.

"No," said the King. "No one has attacked the palace. My people have no reason to attack me. They have peaceful happy lives here in the kingdom. Also an attack would be difficult. The palace guards are very skilled in martial arts[7]. Nobody can pass them and enter[8] the palace." Then the King looked deep into Tom's eyes. "Why do you ask?"

Tom felt himself go very red[9]. He looked at Mahir. Then he looked back at the King. He wanted to say, "Nothing," but he couldn't lie to this man. "There is a man following Mahir," he said. And he told the King about the man with the scar.

"Thank you for telling me about this man," said the King and he looked sternly[10] at his son. "But don't worry," he said. "Mahir is safe here."

Just then, the carriage stopped. A girl ran down the palace steps to the carriage. She was about fifteen years old. She was slim with long straight shiny black hair and a lovely smile. She was beautiful.

"My sister," said Mahir and he jumped out of the carriage.

"I can't believe you're finally here," said the girl, laughing as Mahir gave her a big hug.

"Come and meet Tom," said Mahir. "Tom," said Mahir, "this is my sister, Tara."

"Hi," said Tom.

"Hello, Tom" said Tara. "It's great to meet you at last! I've heard such a lot about you from Mahir. Come on. Let me show you to your room. There's a big festival[11] tomorrow so we have a lot of work to do. I've made you some masks and your costumes[12] are ready. But you need to try them on[13]," she continued excitedly.

---

1 pass by 經過
2 capital [ˈkæpətl] (a.) 首要的
3 realize [ˈrɪəˌlaɪz] (v.) 了解到
4 pollution [pəˈluʃən] (n.) 污染
5 traffic jam 塞車
6 slope [slop] (n.) 坡
7 martial art [ˈmɑrʃəl ɑrt] 武術

8 enter [ˈɛntɚ] (v.) 進入
9 go red 臉紅
10 sternly [ˈstɝnlɪ] (adv.) 嚴厲地
11 festival [ˈfɛstəvl̩] (n.) 節慶活動
12 costume [ˈkɑstjum] (n.) 服裝；戲裝
13 try on 試穿

"Remember," called the Queen, "dinner is at 8 o'clock in the red dining hall."

They walked up the steps and Tom followed. They walked through a gateway[1] and into a courtyard full of orange and yellow flowers.

"This is the Courtyard of the Sun," said Mahir. The sun symbolizes[2] happiness in our kingdom. When you walk through this courtyard, you are given happiness."

They walked through another door into another courtyard. The flowers in this courtyard were all blue.

"This is the Courtyard of the Sky. In our kingdom, a blue sky symbolizes peace and tranquility[3]. When somebody in the palace feels angry, they come and sit in this courtyard. They sit here until their anger goes. When they leave here, they feel calm," said Tara.

They walked through another door into a third courtyard. In this courtyard, all the flowers were white.

"This is the Courtyard of Snow. In our kingdom, snow symbolizes truth. When you walk through this courtyard, you're reminded of[4] the importance of truth," said Mahir. "Happiness, Peace and Truth are the three most important values in the Kingdom of the Snow Leopard."

---

1 gateway [ˈgetˌwe] (n.) 入口處
2 symbolize [ˈsɪmbḷˌaɪz] (v.) 象徵
3 tranquility [trænˈkwɪlətɪ] (n.) 平靜
4 be reminded of 使回想起
5 decorate [ˈdɛkəˌret] (v.) 裝飾
6 corridor [ˈkɔrɪdɚ] (n.) 走廊
7 swing [swɪŋ] (v.)（門在軸上）擺動
　（動態三態：swing; swung; swung）
8 bedspread [ˈbɛdˌsprɛd] (n.) 床罩
9 cushion [ˈkuʃən] (n.) 墊子
10 balcony [ˈbælkənɪ] (n.) 陽臺
11 ribbon [ˈrɪbən] (n.) 帶狀物

COLORS

- What's your favorite color? What feeling does it give when you look at it? What do these colors symbolize to you? Discuss with a partner.
- Write an adjective to go with each color.

  White   Green   Black   Red   Blue   Yellow

Two monks in orange robes opened the golden door in front of them and the three teenagers walked into the palace. Tom had expected the palace to be richly decorated[5], but it wasn't. The walls were white and the floors were stone. They walked up some stairs and down a long corridor[6]. At the end of the corridor, there were two doors.

"This is your room," said Tara and she swung[7] open the first door.

There was a large wooden bed in the room. It was covered with an orange bedspread[8] and lots of orange and gold cushions[9]. Another door led into a white-tiled bathroom. There were two more doors leading out onto a large balcony[10]. The balcony looked out over the forest and the city below. Tom stood and looked out across the pretty red-tiled roofs. Ribbons[11] of wood smoke rose from the chimneys. Tom watched as the smoke rose above the trees, and melted into the blue sky above. He felt happy.

 "Come on," said Mahir. "I'll show you my room."

Mahir's room was bigger than Tom's. But it was not like a teenager's room. There were no posters[1] on the white walls. There was no desk with a computer on it and no TV. Hanging on the wall were three wooden masks.

"What are those?" asked Tom.

"They're for the festival tomorrow," said Tara. "I made them for us. It's taken me days to make them. I wanted them to be really special because it's Tom's first festival."

Tara took down the first mask. It was a golden dragon's face with large red eyes.

"Of course, this mask is for you, Mahir. It is customary[2] for the eldest son of the King to wear a dragon costume to the Golden Festival of Light," she explained to Tom as she handed the mask to Mahir.

Then she took down the second mask. "And this is your mask, Tom," she said and handed him the mask. "This is the snow leopard. Legends[3] say that the snow leopard rescued[4] Princess Kia from a terrible death."

"Who was Princess Kia?" asked Tom.

"She was one of our ancestors[5]," said Tara. "She was a very brave and wise woman. One day, she heard that one of her farmers had lost his yaks[6]. Somebody had stolen them. She decided to go and speak to the administrators[7] of the region about the problem. The administrators for each region live and work in a castle. These castles are usually on a hill or mountain top. While Princess Kia was riding up to the castle, it started to snow. It snowed very heavily and she got lost. Her horse stumbled[8] and fell. It was icy cold and she lost consciousness[9]. While she was unconscious[10], she had a dream. A powerful animal with snow-white fur came and carried her on its back up the icy mountain paths and left her at the gates of the castle. When she woke up, she was in a bed in the castle. They told her that they had found her outside the castle gates. 'The snow leopard saved my life', she said."

---

1 poster [ˈpostə] (n.) 海報
2 customary [ˈkʌstəmˌɛrɪ] (a.) 合乎習俗的
3 legend [ˈlɛdʒənd] (n.) 傳說
4 rescue [ˈrɛskju] (v.) 營救
5 ancestor [ˈænsɛstə] (n.) 祖先
6 yak [jæk] (n.) 犛牛
7 administrator [ədˈmɪnəˌstretə] (n.) 行政官員
8 stumble [ˈstʌmbl] (v.) 絆倒
9 consciousness [ˈkɑnʃəsnɪs] (n.) 意識
10 unconscious [ʌnˈkɑnʃəs] (a.) 不省人事的

"It's just a story," said Mahir, "but many people believe that when a good person is in danger a snow leopard will come to rescue them. The snow leopard is a symbol of strength and courage."

Tom took the white mask with the silver spots[1] and the emerald[2] green eyes. "Thank you very much, Tara. It's beautiful," he said.

Then she took down the third mask. "This is my mask," she said.

It was the face of a beautiful woman. It too had emerald green eyes.

"This is the mask of Princess Kia," said Tara. "Let's hope that you don't have to rescue me tomorrow night," she laughed.

But Tom felt a cold chill[3] when she said the words and a shiver[4] ran down his spine[5]. "Something bad is going to happen tomorrow night," he thought. "I can feel it."

"Look at the time," said Mahir. "It's nearly 8 o'clock. We'd better[6] go down for dinner."

Tom pushed the uneasy thoughts to the back of his mind and followed Mahir and Tara out of the room. They were laughing about something and soon Tom was laughing too.

Dinner was hot! Tom was sweating. "This curry's really hot," he said. "I've never sweated so much before."

"It's the chili pepper[7]," said Tara. "People in our country say, 'It is not worth eating unless you sweat.' But I asked the chef[8] to put less chili in yours."

---

1 spot [spɑt] (n.) 斑點
2 emerald [ˈɛmərəld] (a.) 翠綠色的
3 chill [tʃɪl] (n.) 寒冷
4 shiver [ˈʃɪvə] (n.) 顫抖
5 spine [spaɪn] (n.) 脊椎
6 had better 最好做某事
7 chili pepper 辣椒
8 chef [ʃɛf] (n.) 廚師

"You mean yours is hotter?" said Tom in horror.

"Yes," said Tara and she laughed.

"This is hotter than any Indian curry[1]," said Tom.

And he looked down the long wooden table. All the monks, all the guards and all the palace staff[2] were there. Everybody was sweating but they were all eating happily.

"This is a special dish," said Tara. "It is made from yoghurt cheese. The yoghurt cheese is fried with butter and sugar and then we add red chili pepper."

"Is all the food this hot?" asked Tom.

"Yes, it is. We even eat chili for breakfast. We make a cereal[3] with corn, butter, sugar and chili peppers," said Tara.

Tom ate a large spoonful of rice. "At least the rice isn't hot," he thought. And he took another spoonful. Then he had a drink.

"That's butter tea," said Tara. "We usually drink butter tea or wine or beer made from rice with the meal."

The tea was very sweet. It tasted of caramel[4]. Tom liked it. "Do people eat meat[5] here?" he asked.

"Some people eat meat. They eat yak meat. But most people in the kingdom are vegetarians[6]. We don't eat much meat here in the palace. We only eat it when we have foreign guests or on very special occasions[7]," said Tara. "We don't like killing animals for food."

Just then, the King stood up and he made a speech. "I have a special announcement[8] to make," he said. "The archery competition[9] will start at 8 o'clock tomorrow morning. And this year, my daughter, Tara, will compete[10]."

Tara gasped[11] in excitement. Then she stood up and gave a little bow. Her father smiled at her and everybody clapped[12].

"I wish you success," said her father.

"Thank you, Father," she said and sat down. "I can't believe it! I didn't think he would let me compete because I was too young."

"Compete in what?" asked Tom.

"The archery competition tomorrow morning," said Mahir. "It's a very important competition. People from all over the country will compete. As I told you before, archery is our national sport."

"Yes, I know," said Tom. "You win the school archery competition every year. Nobody else stands a chance[13]."

"I can't help it," said Mahir. "You all need to practice more."

COMPETITION

- Should men and women compete together? Which sports could they compete against each other in? Discuss the sports below:

  ⓐ football　ⓑ martial arts　ⓒ running　ⓓ skating
  ⓔ skiing　ⓕ swimming　ⓖ weightlifting　ⓗ wrestling

1　curry [ˋkɝɪ] (n.) 咖喱
2　staff [stæf] (n.) 工作人員
3　cereal [ˋsɪrɪəl] (n.) 麥片
4　caramel [ˋkærəml̩] (n.) 焦糖
5　meat [mit] (n.) 肉
6　vegetarian [͵vɛdʒəˋtɛrɪən] (n.) 素食者
7　occasion [əˋkeʒən] (n.) 場合

8　announcement [əˋnaʊnsmənt] (n.) 宣布
9　competition [͵kɑmpəˋtɪʃən] (n.) 競賽
10　compete [kəmˋpit] (v.) 比賽
11　gasp [ɡræsp] (v.) 倒抽一口氣
12　clap [klæp] (v.) 鼓掌
13　stand a chance 有希望成功

"So why is Tara so excited about competing tomorrow?"

"She'll be the youngest person to compete," said Mahir. "And it's her first big competition. Here, men and women compete in the same competition. We don't have separate men's and women's competitions."

"Really?" said Tom. "I think that's cool. Hey, but what about you? Are you competing tomorrow?"

"Yes, of course," said Mahir.

"Then, she doesn't stand a chance," said Tom.

"I'm not so sure about that. We'll see," said Mahir. "She's very good."

The King was making another speech. "The festival tomorrow will start at 7 o'clock in the evening. As soon as the archery competition is over everyone must get ready. We'll meet in the Courtyard of the Sun and we'll leave at 1 o'clock," he said. "Now, I wish you good night. Tomorrow will be a long and busy day." He bowed. Then the Queen stood up and bowed. Everybody stood up and bowed. Then the King and Queen left the dining hall.

Mahir explained everything to Tom.

"But why are we leaving so early?" asked Tom.

"The festival is in the Castle of Snow," explained Mahir. "The castle is high up in the mountains, so it will be a long and difficult journey."

"How will we get there?" asked Tom.

---

1 take aim 瞄準
2 fire [faɪr] (v.) 射擊
3 whiz [hwɪz] (v.) 颼颼掠過
4 mark [mɑrk] (n.) 靶子

"On horseback," replied Mahir.

"You've got to be kidding!" said Tom, worried. "I've never ridden a horse before."

"Don't worry," said Mahir. "You can ride on the back of my horse."

"I don't think I can sleep tonight," said Tara. "I'm too excited."

"Well, I feel tired," said Tom. "I think it's time for bed."

"Me too," said Mahir. "It's been a long day."

The next morning, Tom woke early. He walked out onto the balcony and he saw Tara in the garden below. She had her bow and arrow with her. Tom watched her for a few minutes as she carefully took aim[1] and fired[2]. The arrow whizzed[3] through the air and hit a small red mark[4] on a tree about a hundred meters away.

"Wow," she's good," thought Tom.

Just then she looked up and smiled at Tom. She waved at him and he waved back.

Then there was a knock on the door. Tom opened it and Mahir stood there. He was wearing a yellow and gold gho and he was carrying a mediaeval[1]-style helmet[2] and his bow and arrows.

"You look like a knight[3] from the Middle Ages," said Tom.

"It's not like our school sports kit, is it?" laughed Mahir. "Here, feel the weight of this helmet. The sports kit[4] is better."

Tom took the gold helmet. "Yes, that *is* heavy," he said, and he tried it on. "How do I look?"

"It doesn't really go with jeans[5]," said Mahir.

"No, and speaking of jeans—can you help me into my gho? I can't put it on by myself."

"You'll have to learn," said Mahir. "I can't dress you every day."

That morning, breakfast was in a small room. There was just Tom and Mahir. They sat on cushions on the floor around a low table. A monk brought a large bowl of the chili porridge, some corn bread and some butter tea on a big round tray[6].

"Where is everybody?" asked Tom.

"They've already eaten," said Mahir. "We usually eat breakfast at sunrise here in the palace."

"You didn't tell me that last night," said Tom.

"I know you don't like early mornings," said Mahir. "You can never get up at school."

---

1 mediaeval [ˌmidɪˈivl] (a.) 中世紀的
2 helmet [ˈhɛlmɪt] (n.) 頭盔
3 knight [naɪt] (n.) 騎士
4 kit [kɪt] (n.) 成套的工具

5 jeans [dʒinz] (n.)〔複〕牛仔褲
6 tray [tre] (n.) 托盤
7 on fire 著火
8 get used to 習慣於

"School's different," said Tom. Then he ate a small spoonful of porridge. "Oh it's not too hot . . . argh!" The hot chili burned his tongue and the back of his throat. "My mouth's on fire[7]!" said Tom and he ate a large piece of corn bread. "I don't think I'll ever get used to[8] this hot food," he said.

"You will," said Mahir. "By the end of the holiday, you won't think it's hot at all. And when you go home, you'll put chili pepper on your hamburgers!"

The door opened and Tara came in. "Hurry up, you two," she said. "The ceremony[9] is going to start in ten minutes." She was wearing a purple and gold kira and she was carrying her gold helmet and her bow and arrows.

"Have you had enough to eat?" Mahir asked Tom.

"Yes, I'm full," said Tom.

"Then let's go," said Mahir.

And he led them through a maze[10] of corridors to the back of the palace. Finally, they came to a large room, which was full of people.

"All the competitors[11] have to wait in this room," said Mahir. "You can go with my brothers. You can sit in the pagoda[12] with my family. Tara and I will stay here."

Mahir took Tom over to where his brothers were standing. "Tom will come and sit with you," he said and he introduced them all.

9 ceremony [ˈsɛrəˌmonɪ] (n.) 典禮
10 maze [mez] (n.) 迷宮
11 competitor [kəmˈpɛtətəʳ] (n.) 競爭者
12 pagoda [pəˈgodə] (n.) 塔；亭子；棚子

Mahir's brothers were all younger than him. The youngest one, Sami, who was six, came and took Tom's hand. "You can sit next to me," he said.

Then he led Tom outside. Outside there was a huge grass[1] field with grass steps around three sides. People were sitting on brightly colored cushions on the grass steps. They walked to the far end of the field, where the King and Queen were sitting. They were sitting on chairs in a pagoda.

The King and Queen stood and bowed to Tom and Tom bowed back.

"You will sit with me," said the King and he pointed to the chair next to him. Tom went and sat down. Sami sat on a cushion next to his mother's chair.

"Tom," said the King, "you will tell me if you see that man with the scar again."

"Yes, of course," said Tom.

"Mahir will not tell me," said the King. "He thinks that he can look after himself." The King was speaking very quietly in English. "I have found out who he is. He is a journalist[2] and he lives in America. He has no criminal[3] record, but he may be dangerous. He has written a lot of articles for magazines and newspapers about our kingdom, so he knows a lot about us." The King's voice was very serious now. "Tom, Mahir's life could be in danger. You must tell me if he comes near my son again."

"Yes, Your Majesty[4]," said Tom. "Of course, I'll tell you."

Suddenly, there was a loud clash[5] of cymbals[6].

"Aha, I think the competition is about to begin," said the King.

There was another clash of cymbals and then the competitors walked out onto the field. Everybody clapped. The competitors marched[7] in time[8] to a drumbeat[9]. They stopped in front of the royal pagoda and bowed to the King and Queen.

The King stood and bowed back. "Let the competition begin!" he said.

There was a huge cheer[10] from the crowd. The competitors sat on benches on either side of the royal pagoda.

The names of the first two competitors were called, and they walked out onto the field. There were two targets[11]. Three dragons were painted on the targets: a black dragon with a blue eye, a red dragon with a golden eye and a golden dragon with a red eye.

The competitors had to hit the golden eye of the red dragon first and then the red eye of the golden dragon. It was bad luck to hit the blue eye of the black dragon. Each competitor fired two arrows. The competitors raised[12] their first arrows and fired. Two men ran to check the scores[13]. Then they ran and gave the arrows to the competitors.

Many people hit the golden eye of the red dragon, but nobody hit the red eye.

1 grass [græs] (n.) 草地
2 journalist [ˋdʒɝnəlɪst] (n.) 新聞記者
3 criminal [ˋkrɪmənḷ] (a.) 犯罪的
4 Majesty [ˋmædʒɪstɪ] (n.) 〔大寫〕陛下
5 clash [klæʃ] (n.) 碰撞聲
6 cymbal [ˋsɪmbḷ] (n.) 鐃鈸
7 march [mɑrtʃ] (v.) 前進
8 in time 及時
9 drumbeat [ˋdrʌm͵bit] (n.) 鼓聲
10 cheer [tʃɪr] (n.) 歡呼
11 target [ˋtɑrgɪt] (n.) 靶
12 raise [rez] (v.) 舉起
13 score [skor] (n.) 得分

Then, it was Tara's turn. She walked confidently[1] onto the field. She fired the first arrow and hit the golden eye of the red dragon. The crowd cheered. Then she fired the second arrow and hit the red eye of the golden dragon.

She collected her arrows and then turned and bowed to the King. The crowds continued to cheer.

Then it was Mahir's turn. He gave Tom a little wave as he walked onto the field. He looked cool and confident.

He fired the first arrow and hit the golden eye of the red dragon. The crowd cheered and the musicians[2] beat the drums loudly. Then Mahir fired the second arrow. A nervous whisper[3] passed through the crowd, then there was silence. Nobody moved and nobody spoke.

"Mahir has hit the blue eye of the black dragon," thought Tom.

Tom turned and looked at the King. His face was pale and his hands gripped[4] the arms of his chair.

Mahir was still standing on the field. He was staring[5] at the target. Tara ran onto the field and took her brother's hand. She led him off the field.

"Mahir has never hit the blue eye before," said the King.

"If he's never hit it before, why did he hit it today?" Tom wondered and he didn't enjoy the rest of the competition. He wanted to speak to Mahir but he couldn't. He had to wait until the end of the competition.

---

1 confidently [ˈkɑnfədəntlɪ] (adv.) 自信地
2 musician [mjuˈzɪʃən] (n.) 樂師
3 whisper [ˈhwɪspɚ] (n.) 私語

4 grip [grɪp] (v.) 緊握
5 stare [stɛr] (v.) 盯；凝視

Finally, the competition ended and they announced the winner. It was Princess Tara. She walked up to the pagoda and her father gave her a small statue[1] of a golden dragon. She held it up for the crowds to see. They cheered and clapped the princess. Tom could see that she was very popular.

The other prizes were awarded[2] and then Tara led the competitors off the field. The King and Queen and the royal family followed the competitors. Everybody else remained sitting.

Tom looked around for Mahir, but he couldn't see him. Tara came over to him. "Where's Mahir?" asked Tom. "He's not here. Is he okay?"

"Don't worry," said Tara. "I know where he is." Then Tara led Tom to a small walled garden. Mahir was sitting on the grass under an orange tree.

"He always comes here when he is upset[3]," whispered Tara.

Tom could see why. It was very peaceful in the garden. Tom and Tara sat down on the grass next to Mahir. They sat in silence for a moment.

Then Mahir said, "Congratulations, Tara. I'm very proud of you." And he gave her a big hug.

"You were my teacher," said Tara. "I learnt everything from you."

"Thank you," said Mahir. "Now you and Tom should go and get ready for the festival."

"Aren't you coming?" asked Tara, upset.

"No," said Mahir. "I want to be alone for a while."

Just then, the King walked into the garden. "Tara, you and Tom go and get your costumes on. I will talk to my son."

PROBLEMS

- When you are upset, who do you usually talk to?
  - a A parent
  - b A friend
  - c A teacher
- What kind of problems do you talk about with:
  - a a teacher
  - b your mother
  - c your father
  - d a friend
- Share with a partner.

Tara squeezed[4] her brother's hand. Then she got up. Tom got up, too. And they left the garden. "Is the King angry?" asked Tom.

"No," said Tara and she smiled. "He is never angry. He'll talk to Mahir and he'll convince[5] him to come to the festival with us this afternoon."

Back in his room, Tom picked up the mask and studied it. He ran his fingers over the finely carved[6] wood and traced[7] round the beautiful emerald green eyes. "What would it be like to be a leopard?"

He thought about its strength and the power of its legs. He imagined it moving gracefully across the snow. Then he held the mask to his face and looked in the mirror.

---

1 statue [ˈstætʃʊ] (n.) 雕像
2 award [əˈwɔrd] (v.) 頒獎
3 upset [ʌpˈsɛt] (a.) 心煩的
4 squeeze [skwiz] (v.) 緊握

5 convince [kənˈvɪns] (v.) 說服
6 carved [kɑrvd] (a.) 雕刻的
7 trace [tres] (v.) 細摸輪廓

"There is magic in this mask. I can feel it," he thought. Then he felt a sudden powerful surge[1] of energy race through his veins[2].

"The mask is making me feel stronger," he thought and he jumped into the air. His legs felt strong and it was easy to jump. He jumped again and again and each time, he jumped higher.

"I wish Mahir was here," he thought. "He could explain it to me."

Then he felt a presence[3] in the room and he turned and faced the door. A figure[4] stood in the doorway[5]. Tom stared into the face of the golden dragon.

"Mahir," said Tom, happily. "You've changed your mind. You're coming."

"Yes," said Mahir and he took off the mask. "My father told me a story and he made me feel better."

"What was the story?" asked Tom and he took off the leopard mask.

"Many years ago, my father was a competitor in the archery competition. Actually it was his first competition."

"Don't tell me," interrupted Tom, "he hit the blue eye."

"Yes," said Mahir. "He hit the blue eye. And like me, he was very upset. After the competition, his father talked to him. He told him to think positive[6] thoughts and the bad luck would go away. He did as his father told him and nothing bad happened. Then one day, he rode up into the mountains and there was a very bad snowstorm. It turned into a blizzard[7] and he couldn't see anything. Soon, he was lost. He knew that he had to find his way home before dark. If he stayed out in the snow all night, he would die. Then he saw a piece of orange cloth in the snow. He got off his horse and he started to dig the snow around the cloth with his hands. He found the body of a monk. Fortunately the monk was still alive. My father put the monk on his horse. He knew now that he must be near a castle. The monk would not walk far in those thin orange robes. An hour later, he found the castle."

"And did the monk survive?" asked Tom.

"Yes, he did," said Mahir. "He came to live in the palace with my father. They're good friends now. My father said that his bad luck was the monk's good luck. He got lost but he saved the monk's life. He said that I will have bad luck but it will bring good luck to someone else. And the good luck will be stronger than the bad."

1 surge [sɝdʒ] (n.) 澎湃
2 vein [ven] (n.) 血管
3 presence [ˋprɛzn̩s] (n.) 在場
4 figure [ˋfɪgjɚ] (n.) 人影
5 doorway [ˋdor͵we] (n.) 門口
6 positive [ˋpɑzətɪv] (a.) 正面的
7 blizzard [ˋblɪzɚd] (n.) 暴風雪

"I hope so," said Tom.

"And now," said Mahir, "get dressed or our bad luck will be to miss the festival."

Mahir lifted a silver and white gho from the wardrobe[1] and helped Tom into it.

Later, when Mahir and Tom walked into the Courtyard of the Sun, everybody was there. There were tigers and horses, red and black dragons, heroes and demons.

"You're late," said a voice behind Tom. He turned and he saw Tara.

Tara was wearing a silver kira decorated with tiny blue flowers made with beads. Her long dark hair hung down her back and was threaded with little silver beads[2] that sparkled in the sunlight. She was holding her mask. She was very beautiful.

"Will you rescue me?" asked Tara, jokingly.

"Of course," said Tom.

"Whatever the danger?" she asked.

"Whatever the danger!" said Tom.

"Promise?"

"Yes, promise," said Tom.

There was a clash of cymbals and the King and Queen rode through the gates. Mahir was following them. He rode over to Tom on a huge black stallion[3]. "Are you ready?" he asked Tom and he jumped down.

---

1 wardrobe ['wɔrd,rob] (n.) 衣櫥
2 bead [bid] (n.) 有孔的小珠子
3 stallion ['stæljən] (n.) 牡馬；種馬

Tom didn't feel ready at all. He couldn't ride and he wasn't looking forward to the journey.

Mahir helped him up into the saddle[1]. Then he jumped up himself. They put their masks into a bag, which hung from the saddle. Mahir gave the horse a little kick with his heels and they trotted[2] out of the courtyard and went down the long driveway.

Tom hung on tightly and closed his eyes. He soon became used to the movement of the horse and began to enjoy the speed.

"I haven't ridden for a long time," Mahir shouted into the wind. "When we get up into the mountains, we will have to go slowly, but now we can race the wind." And that is exactly what it felt like. They were racing the wind. Tom looked back and saw the royal party[3] far behind.

Then he saw a white horse. It was cantering[4] along at high speed. Tom knew it was Tara. She looked fearless and brave.

"How could I ever rescue her?" Tom thought. "She'll probably have to rescue me."

The horse slowed into a trot as they began to climb steeply[5] and the road began to narrow until it became nothing more than a track[6].

"Now I know why they don't have cars here," Tom thought. "There's nowhere to drive them. No smooth[7] wide motorways[8] to speed along in big fast cars." He wondered if Mahir missed them. "Don't you miss cars?" he asked.

1 saddle [ˈsædl̩] (n.) 馬鞍
2 trot [trɑt] (v.) (n.) 小跑；快步
3 party [ˈpɑrtɪ] (n.) 一行人
4 canter [ˈkæntɚ] (v.) （馬）慢跑
（速度介於 gallop 與 trot 之間）
5 steeply [ˈstiplɪ] (adv.) 險峻地
6 track [træk] (n.) 小路
7 smooth [smuð] (a.) 平坦的
8 motorway [ˈmotɚˌwe] (n.) 〔英〕高速公路

"Why would I miss them? In England you either sit in a long tail[1] of traffic with smoke billowing[2] from exhaust pipes[3] all around you or you travel at 30 mph[4] in fear of being caught by a speed camera. If you're caught speeding three times by the speed cameras, you lose your driving license[5]. Then you have to travel by bus. No, thank you. I prefer being here. There are no traffic jams here and you can ride as fast as you like."

"So if your dad gave you a red Ferrari for your 18th birthday, you would give it back," said Tom.

There was silence for a moment and then Mahir laughed. "My father would never give me a Ferrari for my 18th. But if he did, I would be the happiest boy on Earth."

Just then, they turned a bend[6] in the track. "Don't look down," shouted Mahir.

Of course, Tom looked down and to his horror, he saw a deep bottomless ravine[7]. Tom felt the same adrenalin rush[8] as he had felt on his first roller-coaster[9] ride. "That's a long way to fall," he said. "I hope this horse knows what it's doing!"

"Don't worry," said Mahir. "I've ridden up here hundreds of times."

Tom looked across at the snowy mountain peaks ahead of them. "We're really high up now, aren't we?" he said.

---

1 tail [tel] (n.) 尾狀物
2 billow [ˋbɪlo] (v.) 波濤洶湧
3 exhaust pipe [ɪgˋzɔst paɪp] 排氣管
4 mph 每小時英里數 (= miles per hour)
5 driving license [ˋdraɪvɪŋ ˋlaɪsn̩s] 駕駛執照
6 bend [bɛnd] (n.) 轉彎
7 ravine [rəˋvin] (n.) 深谷

8 adrenalin rush [ædˋrɛnl̩ɪn rʌʃ] 腎上腺素激升
9 roller-coaster [ˋroləˋkostə] (n.) 雲霄飛車
10 sea level 海平面
11 echo [ˋɛko] (v.) 回盪
12 catch up with 趕上
13 edge [ɛdʒ] (n.) 邊緣

"Not really," replied Mahir. "We're 3,000 meters above sea level[10]. We're going to climb another 1,000 meters to the castle."

"I've never been anywhere so high before," said Tom amazed.

"Hello, there!" shouted Tara and her voice echoed[11] back and forth across the mountains. She had caught up with[12] them.

"Hi, not far to go now," Mahir shouted back.

Then they turned another bend in the track and Tom saw the castle. The castle was built on the side of the next mountain. "Is that where we're going?" he asked.

"Yes," said Mahir. "It's amazing, isn't it?"

"But how do we get into it?" asked Tom. "It's right on the edge[13] of the mountain."

"You'll see when we get there," said Mahir.

They rode for another two hours. The castle was always in sight but it was always far away. Then suddenly there was a sharp twist in the narrow track. They rode round it and onto a wide road—not wide compared to a motorway, but very wide compared to the narrow track.

The huge wooden gates of the castle stood in front of them. Two men on horseback stood on either side of the gates. They were dressed from head to toe in gold. The gates were open and Tom could see a blur[1] of rich colors inside. The festival had begun. He could hear the beating of drums and the sound of pipes.

Tom felt a thrill[2] of excitement as they dismounted[3] from their horses. Two men came running up to them and led the horses away. Tara, Tom and Mahir put on their masks and walked through the thick stone archway[4] into the courtyard beyond.

It wasn't a rock concert, but it was just as exciting. Everywhere he looked, people were wearing masks. Even the monks in their orange robes were wearing masks. There were tigers with thick black and orange stripes[5], small pointed ears and huge green eyes and there were monkeys and horses and birds.

"Each animal symbolizes a different quality," said Tara. "The tiger symbolizes strength and the monkey symbolizes wisdom[6], the bird symbolizes freedom and the horse symbolizes friendship."

"In your culture, you treat animals as inferior[7]," said Mahir. "You love them, but you don't think they've got anything to teach you. Here we respect them. We know that they have greater powers than we do."

"What do you mean?" asked Tom.

"Animals listen to nature. They can sense[8] things that humans can't sense. They know when there's going to be a storm or an earthquake, but we don't."

Just then there was a clash of cymbals and everybody stopped and turned towards the archway.

"The King and Queen are here," whispered Tara.

The King and Queen walked through the archway and everybody bowed. They were not wearing masks.

"Why aren't they wearing masks?" Tom asked.

"They come as themselves," said Tara. "As the King and Queen, they symbolize the peace and happiness of our country."

The King and Queen sat on a raised platform at the far end of the courtyard. They sat down on their thrones. As they sat down, there was a clash of steel[9] on steel, and Tom turned to see a group of warriors[10] enter the castle. They marched to the center of the courtyard.

---

1 blur [blɜ] (n.) 模糊
2 thrill [θrɪl] (n.) 顫慄
3 dismount [dɪsˋmaʊnt] (v.) 下馬
4 archway [ˋɑrtʃ͵we] (n.) 拱門；拱道
5 stripe [straɪp] (n.) 條紋

6 wisdom [ˋwɪzdəm] (n.) 智慧
7 inferior [ɪnˋfɪrɪɚ] (a.) 次等的
8 sense [sɛns] (v.) 感覺
9 steel [stil] (n.) 鋼鐵
10 warrior [ˋwɔrɪɚ] (n.) 武士；戰士

ANIMALS

- How are animals treated in your country? Is any animal considered special?
- Are there any legends about animals? Discuss with a partner.

The crowds moved silently out of their way.

"The first dance of the evening is a sword[1] dance," said Mahir. "These men are the best swordsmen[2] in the country. They practice for five or six hours every day."

"I thought you said people didn't fight with weapons[3] in this country," said Tom.

"They don't," said Mahir, "but all our warriors are skilled swordsmen. Swordsmanship[4] is an art form. It requires skill and concentration."

As they watched the swordsmen, the sun began to set[5]. The pink sky turned to grey, then black until night fell. The monks lit lanterns all around the castle walls. The lanterns glowed[6] and flickered[7] and sent shadows racing across the dark courtyard. The masks with their huge eyes looked scary[8] in this light.

Tom turned to talk to Tara, but she wasn't there. He looked around, but he couldn't see her.

1 sword [sord] (n.) 劍
2 swordsman [ˋsordzmən] (n.) 劍客;軍人
3 weapon [ˋwɛpən] (n.) 武器
4 swordsmanship [ˋsordzmənʃɪp] (n.) 劍術
5 set [sɛt] (v.)(日、月等) 落下
6 glow [glo] (v.) 發光
7 flicker [ˋflɪkɚ] (v.) 閃爍;搖曳
8 scary [ˋskɛrɪ] (a.) 嚇人的
9 metal [ˋmɛtl] (n.) 金屬製品
10 sapphire [ˋsæfaɪr] (n.) 藍寶石;青玉

Then he saw it—metal[9] on the stone floor. He pushed his way through the crowds and bent down to pick it up. It was one of Tara's silver and sapphire[10] dragon earrings[11]. He felt a hand on his shoulder. His heart began to beat very fast. He stood up quickly and then he let out a sigh of relief[12] when he saw the golden dragon mask.

"Oh, thank goodness, it's you, Mahir," he said.

"Come on," said Mahir. "We have to go."

"Go where?" asked Tom. "Are you okay? Your voice sounds a bit strange. Is something wrong?"

"Don't ask questions. Just follow me," said Mahir.

His grasp[13] on Tom's arm was strong. His fingers dug into Tom's arm and Tom could sense his fear.

"We have to go," he repeated urgently[14].

"Where's Tara?" asked Tom with a note of panic in his voice. "I found her earring on the ground. Have you seen her? Is she all right?"

Mahir didn't reply. He continued to pull Tom through the crowded courtyard towards the archway. Tom began to walk more quickly. He knew something was wrong. Something had upset Mahir. He had to be patient. He had to stop asking questions. Mahir would explain everything soon.

Now they were outside the castle. There was a strong wind and it was icy cold. Tom could only see a few steps in front of him. He couldn't see the ravine but he knew it was close.

---

11 earring [ˋɪr͵rɪŋ] (n.) 耳環
12 relief [rɪˋlif] (n.) 鬆口氣
13 grasp [græsp] (n.) 緊抓
14 urgently [ˋɝdʒəntlɪ] (adv.) 急迫地

Mahir walked close to the castle wall and Tom walked next to him. He could hear the horses neighing[1] in the stables[2] and the wind howling[3]. Eventually, Mahir stopped and he pushed open a wooden door in front of them. Somebody shone a torch[4] in Tom's face. He couldn't see anything.

"What's happening?" he called out.

Mahir pushed him into the room and then closed the heavy wooden door.

When his eyes got used to the light, Tom saw that there were three other people in the room. Near the doorway, there was a man with a gun and sitting on the floor in the far corner were two people in masks. Tom recognized the masks immediately— the golden dragon and Princess Kia.

Tom turned round to face the masked man behind him. The man pulled off[5] the golden dragon mask and laughed. "The perfect disguise[6]," said the man. "Only one person is allowed to wear the golden dragon mask."

"It's you," said Tom. "We saw you outside the school gates and in the airport. You've been following Mahir."

"Sit down and shut up," said the man.

"Do as he says, Tom," said Mahir from the corner.

Tom looked from Mahir to the man. Then he saw the gun pointed at him and he went to sit down. The other man came and tied his arms behind his back and then tied his feet together. The thick rope cut into his wrists.

---

1 neigh [ne] (v.) （馬）嘶　　4 torch [tɔrtʃ] (n.) 火把
2 stable [ˋstebl] (n.) 馬廄　　5 pull off 脫下；拿掉
3 howl [haʊl] (v.) 怒吼　　6 disguise [dɪsˋgaɪz] (n.) 偽裝

"What do you want from us?" asked Mahir. There was no anger or fear in his voice.

"I want the Shining Star," said the man.

Tara drew in a sharp breath but Mahir remained[1] calm. "You and your father are the only two people in the world who know where it is."

"Then you don't need Tom and Tara," said Mahir calmly. "Let them go and I will take you to the Shining Star."

The man laughed loudly. "Do you think I'm stupid? Do you think I don't know your powers? I've been watching you for months. With one tiny[2] flick[3] of your wrist you can paralyze[4] me," he said.

LOYALTY & FRIENDSHIP

- What are the qualities of a good friend? Discuss with a partner. List them in order of importance.

"These two are staying here. I know you won't try to escape[5] if they're here. You won't put their lives in danger. If I don't return with the Shining Star, my friend here will shoot them. Two silenced shots and your precious sister and your best friend will be dead."

There was a silence. "I will take you to the Shining Star," said Mahir. "But I warn you now, it is a dangerous journey. Are you prepared to face the dangers ahead?"

"I am prepared to face anything for the Shining Star," said the man.

"Very well," said Mahir. "Let's go. I'm sure my father will send a search party for us soon."

"Nobody will miss you. Princess Kia, the snow leopard and the golden dragon are still at the festival," said the man. "My friends are there in your place. They are wearing identical[6] masks. Now, Crown Prince Mahir I'm going to untie[7] you," said the man. "One false move and my friend will shoot the princess."

Mahir looked at his sister. The short stocky[8] man with the shaved[9] head and the mean eyes had one arm around Tara's throat and he was holding a gun to her head with his other hand. Then Mahir turned to Tom and said. "Remember, 'practice makes perfect.' Look after my sister for me."

"That's enough of the chit-chat[10]," said the man with the scar. He went over and cut the ropes that tied Mahir's feet and arms. "Walk to the door with your arms above your head. No sudden moves or your sister dies."

The man tightened his grip[11] around Tara's neck and she squealed[12] in pain.

---

1 remain [rɪˋmen] (v.) 保持
2 tiny [ˋtaɪnɪ] (a.) 微小的
3 flick [flɪk] (n.) 輕打；輕彈
4 paralyze [ˋpærəˏlaɪz] (v.) 使癱瘓
5 escape [əˋskep] (v.) 逃跑
6 identical [aɪˋdɛntɪkl̩] (a.) 完全相同的
7 untie [ʌnˋtaɪ] (v.) 解開
8 stocky [ˋstɑkɪ] (a.) 矮胖的
9 shaved [ʃevd] (a.) 剃光毛髮的
10 chit-chat [ˋtʃɪtˏtʃæt] (n.) 小閒聊
11 grip [grɪp] (n.) 緊握
12 squeal [skwil] (v.) 發出長而尖的叫聲

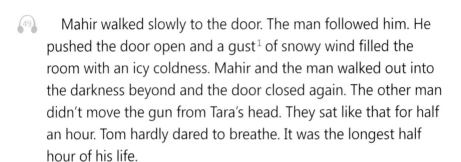

Mahir walked slowly to the door. The man followed him. He pushed the door open and a gust[1] of snowy wind filled the room with an icy coldness. Mahir and the man walked out into the darkness beyond and the door closed again. The other man didn't move the gun from Tara's head. They sat like that for half an hour. Tom hardly dared to breathe. It was the longest half hour of his life.

Finally the man took his arm from around Tara's throat and he went and sat on the other side of the room. The gun was still pointed at them.

"Can we talk?" asked Tom.

The man nodded.

"What's the Shining Star?" asked Tom.

"I don't know exactly," said Tara. "I've never seen it. Only Mahir and my father have ever seen it. But legends say that it is the most precious thing on Earth. It is worth more than all the gold in Asia. Some people say that it's a huge diamond, but I don't know."

Meanwhile Mahir and his kidnapper[2] were struggling[3] to climb up a steep mountain path. Mahir knew every inch of the path but the snow was falling heavily and he couldn't see his usual footholds[4]. Their destination[5] was not far away, but in these conditions[6] it would take them at least two hours to climb there.

Mahir's kidnapper was an experienced climber, but he was finding the climb difficult.

"I could easily escape," thought Mahir. "But then, how could I rescue Tom and Tara?"

The ground was icy and very slippery[7]. Mahir was not wearing the right shoes for climbing, but his feet never slipped[8].

After climbing for an hour, they came to a small cave. The cave was halfway to their destination.

---

1 gust [gʌst] (n.) 一陣強風
2 kidnapper [ˋkɪdnæpɚ] (n.) 綁票者
3 struggle [ˋstrʌgl] (v.) 掙扎
4 foothold [ˋfʊt͵hold] (n.) 踏腳處
5 destination [͵dɛstəˋneʃən] (n.) 目的地
6 conditions [kənˋdɪʃənz] (n.)〔複〕條件
7 slippery [ˋslɪpərɪ] (a.) 滑的
8 slip [slɪp] (v.) 滑倒

"We can stop and rest here for a few minutes," said Mahir.

The man agreed. They sat on the cold stone floor of the cave hugging their knees and staring at the white wall of snow outside.

"What are you going to do with the Shining Star?" asked Mahir.

"I have a friend, a businessman in North America who will pay me a fortune[1] for the diamond."

"I see," said Mahir and he smiled. "How did you hear about the diamond?"

"I'm a journalist and I've written a lot of articles about the Kingdom of the Snow Leopard. You could say I'm an expert[2] on the history and politics[3] of your country and my friend knew that so he invited me to have dinner with him one evening."

The kidnapper paused[4] and thought back to that evening when he first met Jack Sharpe. Jack was wearing a scruffy[5] suit with patches[6] on the elbows. It was hard to imagine that he was one of the richest men in the world.

"When he first asked me to steal the diamond for him, I refused. I have grown to respect your father over the years and I didn't want to steal anything from him. But then I lost my job at the newspaper. They made me redundant[7]. Work was hard to find and the chance to earn a huge fortune became more attractive. Finally, I rang my friend and I agreed to steal the diamond for him."

---

1 fortune [ˈfɔrtʃən] (n.) 財富
2 expert [ˈɛkspɚt] (n.) 專家
3 politics [ˈpɑlətɪks] (n.) 政治
4 pause [pɔz] (v.) 暫停；中斷
5 scruffy [ˈskrʌfɪ] (a.) 破舊的
6 patch [pætʃ] (n.) 補釘
7 redundant [rɪˈdʌndənt] (a.) 被解雇的
8 reflect [rɪˈflɛkt] (v.) 反射

Mahir looked into his kidnapper's eyes for a few moments. "I hope the diamond will not disappoint you," he said coldly. "Now, we should go."

Mahir stood up and then walked out through the wall of white and disappeared. The kidnapper felt a chill inside that was not caused by the snow. The chill was caused by doubt. In those few moments, he had seen the evil of his acts reflected[8] in the boy's eyes. He got up and tried to shake the cold from his bones and the doubt from his mind. Then he followed Mahir.

Once outside the cave, he could just see the heels of the boy's shoes on the rocks above him. He held on tightly to the slippery rocks. He knew that with one false move he could lose his life and his determination[9] to steal the Shining Star returned. And with every step he took, it grew stronger.

Tom and Tara watched the man's eyes droop[10]. He was tired and he was not used to the cold. Hopefully he would fall asleep.

Tara yawned and the man yawned, too. Tom yawned and closed his eyes. Tara closed her eyes, too. Moments later, they heard the thud[11] of the gun as it hit the ground. The man was asleep.

"There's a dagger[12] in the pouch[13] at my waist," whispered Tara. "It's only small, but it's very sharp. Try and get it."

---

9 determination [dɪˌtɜməˈneʃən] (n.) 決心
10 droop [drup] (v.) 低垂
11 thud [θʌd] (n.) 砰的一聲

12 dagger [ˈdæɡɚ] (n.) 短劍；匕首
13 pouch [pautʃ] (n.) 小袋子

Tara was carrying a small golden dagger in a pouch that hung from the cloth belt around her waist. Tom maneuvered[1] himself closer to her and after many attempts, he managed to take the dagger from the pouch. Then he passed the dagger to Tara. They sat with their backs to each other and slowly Tara cut the rope that tied Tom's hands. It seemed to take forever to cut through the thick rope. The man was snoring[2] now, but there was still the danger that he might wake up and take the dagger. Or worse, he might wake up and shoot them.

Once free, Tom cut the rope that tied his feet. Then, he stood up very carefully and he crept towards the man. The man heard him and his eyes shot open. But he didn't see Tom. He saw a powerful animal with huge white paws[3]. Its green eyes glinted[4] in the firelight and its sharp white teeth gleamed[5]. It was a snow leopard.

The man leapt to his feet and pulled a dagger out.

Tom stared at the sharp blade[6]. It was pointed at him. Tom remembered Mahir's words, 'If you believe you can do it, you will do it.'

Tom took a step towards the man. Quickly, he grabbed the man's arm. But the man didn't see Tom, he saw a snow leopard and he lunged[7] at it with his dagger.

Tom moved sideways[8] but the dagger cut his arm. Tom expected to feel pain but he felt none.

---

1 maneuver [mə`nuvɚ] (v.) 巧妙地操縱
2 snore [snor] (v.) 打鼾
3 paw [pɔ] (n.) 爪子
4 glint [glɪnt] (v.) 閃閃發光
5 gleam [glim] (v.) 發微光；閃現
6 blade [bled] (n.) 刀葉
7 lunge [lʌndʒ] (v.) 撲；衝
8 sideways [`saɪd͵wez] (adv.) 向旁邊

"Concentrate," he said to himself. "Concentrate." Then he pressed his finger firmly onto the man's shoulder.

The man felt the sharp claws[1] of the leopard dig into his shoulder. Tom felt the man's limbs[2] stiffen[3]. In one swift[4] movement he twisted and threw the man over his shoulder. He heard the thud as the man hit the ground.

"Get up," he shouted at the man. And he saw the look of horror on the man's face.

"Move now," said Tom, but the man lay still.

"I've done it," said Tom. "I've finally done it."

And he threw the mask up into the air. The man watched as the snow leopard leapt[5] over him and disappeared from the room.

"Tom, we have to go," said Tara. "We haven't got much time."

Quickly Tom ran over and untied Tara.

"Let's get out of here," she said.

"But what about Mahir? Where are they taking him?" asked Tom.

"I don't know," said Tara. "I don't know where they keep the Shining Star. We have to find my father. He's the only other person who knows where it is."

Tom turned the door handle. Then he pushed the door. "The door's locked," he said.

"See if that man has a key," said Tara.

---

1 claw [klɔ] (n.) 爪
2 limb [lɪm] (n.) （四）肢
3 stiffen [ˋstɪfn̩] (v.) 變僵硬
4 swift [swɪft] (a.) 迅速的
5 leap [lip] (v.) 跳躍（動詞三態：leap; leaped/leapt; leaped/leapt）
6 firmly [ˋfɝmlɪ] (adv.) 堅固地
7 cracking [ˋkrækɪŋ] (a.) 重大的

Quickly Tom searched the man's clothes, but he couldn't find a key.

"No, there's no key here," said Tom. "What are we going to do?"

"Stand back," said Tara. She was staring at the door and she was concentrating hard. Then she leapt in the air and kicked the door with her foot. The heavy wooden door shook but it stayed firmly[6] shut. Tara leapt into the air and kicked the door again. There was a huge cracking[7] sound and the door flew outwards. An icy wind blew into the room.

"Wow!" said Tom. "That was pretty cool."

"Come on, Tom," said Tara. "We're free."

"Yes, we're free," thought Tom, as they walked out. "But Mahir's life is still in danger."

Huge snowflakes[1] swirled[2] around them, stinging[3] their faces with their icy coldness.

"I can't see anything," said Tom.

Tara took hold of his hand. "Stay close to the wall," she said. "We can follow it round to the castle gate. "Remember we are very near to the edge of the ravine, so move very carefully. One wrong foot and we could fall over 1,000 meters."

"Thanks, Tara," said Tom. "I feel much happier knowing that."

Then he thought about the journey to the room. "Tara," he said. "When that man brought me to the room, I walked next to him. I didn't know we were so close to the ravine."

"Don't think about that now," said Tara and she held his hand tighter. "We survived and that's all that matters."

Tara and Tom continued to move very slowly around the castle walls.

FEAR

- What are you afraid of? What is your biggest fear? Make a list. Share with a partner.
- Which of these things would you find the most frightening?
  ☐ Being stuck in a broken ski-lift
  ☐ Walking through a forest alone at night
  ☐ Being on a hijacked plane
  ☐ Being stuck in a carriage on the underground

The castle courtyard was empty now. The lanterns still flickered on the walls but everybody was now inside to escape from the snow. The guards were surprised to see Tara and Tom.

"Where's my father?" asked Tara. "Please take us to him immediately."

"Yes, Your Highness[4]," said the guards.

"A man tried to kidnap us. He's tied up in the room next to the stables. Please can you take him to a safer place and keep him under guard[5]."

"Of course," said the guards. And one of them ran off to get some more guards.

Luckily, the King was not with the guests. He was in a room which looked like a library and he was alone.

"Father!" cried Tara when she saw him. And she ran in and hugged him.

"What on earth's the matter?" asked the King.

"It's Mahir," said Tara and the King's face turned pale.

"What's happened to him?" asked the King, his voice calm.

"He's been kidnapped," said Tara.

The King looked over her head at Tom. "Is it the journalist who's been following him?" he asked Tom.

"Yes," said Tom. "It's him."

"Did he say why he was kidnapping Mahir?" asked the King.

"Yes," said Tara. "He wants the Shining Star. Mahir is taking him to the Shining Star."

---

1 snowflake [`sno͵flek] (n.) 雪花
2 swirl [swɝl] (v.) 旋轉
3 sting [stɪŋ] (v.) 刺痛（動態三態：
   sting; stung; stung）
4 Highness [`haɪnɪs] (n.) （大寫）殿下
5 under guard 被看守中

"I see," said the King and he looked thoughtful.

"But, I don't know where they went," said Tara and she told her father the whole story."

"Don't worry, Tara," said her father. "I know where they're going. We can get there before them. They're going to the Temple of the Moon. It's at the top of this mountain. Mahir didn't come into the castle, so I think he has gone up the mountain path. It will take him about two hours in this weather."

"We'll never catch up with them," said Tom.

"There is an underground passage[1] that leads from this castle up to the temple. It will only take us ten minutes to get there along the passage," replied the King.

Just then, a guard entered the room and spoke to the King. The King gave him some instructions[2] and then the guard bowed and left the room.

"I'm coming with you, Father," said Tara.

"And I'm coming too," said Tom.

The King did not argue with them. He wanted to get to the temple before Mahir showed the journalist the Shining Star.

"We must leave now," said the King and he lead them out into the corridor. There was a door at the end of the corridor and a guard opened the door as they approached[3].

They walked into a narrow passageway[4]. In front of them was a line of men carrying lanterns. Tom saw the huge swords that hung from their belts.

"Are those the swordsmen from the festival?" he asked Tara.

"Yes," said Tara. "Nobody who knows of their skills would dare[5] to challenge them. And I think that journalist knows a lot about our kingdom."

The narrow passage climbed steeply and the journey up it was not easy.

When they reached the other end, they walked out into a room with a huge domed[6] ceiling. The ceiling was painted dark blue and it was decorated with hundreds of silver and gold stars. The moon was painted in the center.

The room was full of monks in orange robes who were sitting on mats[7] and chanting. The chanting stopped and a boy in orange robes ran towards them, his footsteps echoing on the stone floor. When he saw the King, he stopped and bowed before him.

"Take me to the Shining Star," said the King.

The boy bowed again and stood up. Tara walked towards her father.

"You can't come with me, Tara," said the King. "You and Tom sit somewhere out of sight and wait for your brother to come."

The boy and the King walked to the front of the temple and disappeared behind a thick embroidered[8] curtain.

"I've never been here before," said Tara and she gazed[9] up at the magnificent[10] ceiling.

---

1 passage [ˋpæsɪdʒ] (n.) 走廊；過道
2 instructions [ɪnˋstrʌkʃənz] (n.)〔複〕指示
3 approach [əˋprotʃ] (v.) 接近
4 passageway [ˋpæsɪdʒ͵we] (n.) 通道
5 dare [dɛr] (v.) 竟敢
6 domed [domd] (a.) 圓屋頂的

7 mat [mæt] (n.) 草蓆；墊子
8 embroidered [ɪmˋbrɔɪdəd] (a.) 繡花的
9 gaze [gez] (v.) 注視
10 magnificent [mægˋnɪfəsənt] (a.) 壯麗的；豪華的

The swordsmen were now sitting on mats with the monks who had begun chanting again. Tara and Tom went and sat down with the monks, too. Tara began to chant, but Tom sat in silence.

Suddenly, a door at the front of the temple creaked[1] open and two white figures stumbled[2] into the temple. The monks continued to chant. They ignored[3] the two figures in the doorway.

Tom saw the gun in the man's hand and he felt his heart racing as the man grabbed Mahir and held one arm around his neck. He watched as the man held the gun to Mahir's head.

"Bring me the Shining Star," he shouted in a cold clear voice, "or I will kill your precious prince!"

A monk walked out from behind the embroidered curtain and said, "I will bring you the Shining Star. Are you ready to see it?"

"Yes," cried the man. "I'm ready."

"Then put your gun down," said the monk.

The man tightened his hold around Mahir's neck and Mahir choked[4].

"Put the gun down and I'll bring you the Shining Star," repeated the monk in a calm clear voice.

The journalist let go of Mahir and he bent down and put the gun on the floor.

The King held open the curtain and a little boy walked into the room. He was about six years old. The King took hold of his hand and together they walked towards the journalist.

"Here is the Shining Star," said the King and the boy took a step forward.

---

1 creak [krik] (v.) 使咯吱咯吱響
2 stumble [ˋstʌmbl̩] (v.) 蹣跚而行
3 ignore [ɪgˋnor] (v.) 不理會
4 choke [tʃok] (v.) 窒息；哽噎

"You're lying," said the journalist and he bent down to pick up the gun again. Nobody moved.

"The Shining Star is the most precious thing on Earth," said the King calmly. "Do you really think the most precious thing on Earth is a diamond? Do you think that the most precious thing on Earth is money?"

SATISFACTION

▪ What is important to you? List the items in order of importance. Say why they are important.
- ☐ Spending time with friends
- ☐ Being healthy
- ☐ Being wealthy
- ☐ Being successful
- ☐ Being popular at school
- ☐ Having trendy clothes
- ☐ Being artistically or musically talented
- ☐ Being good at sport

The journalist stared in horror at the King. Now he knew that the King was not lying. There was no diamond. He dropped the gun and two swordsmen ran and took hold of him by the arms.

"The most precious thing on Earth is life," said the King and he turned and led the little boy back into the room behind the curtain.

Tara ran to Mahir and hugged him. "Are you okay?" she asked.

"I'm cold, but fine," said Mahir and he waved at Tom. Tom ran over to them.

"I guess the kidnapping was your bad luck," said Tom. "But who got the good luck?"

"You and Tara, of course," said Mahir.

"I don't understand," said Tom.

"I do," said Tara. "We were lucky to see the Shining Star. We will be rewarded[1] with long life and happiness."

"Hmm," said Tom. "I'll take your word for it." Then he thought about it for a while and he realized that Tara was right. He was lucky. He learnt a very important lesson today, too.

"Life is very special," he thought.

The holiday came to an end all too quickly. Tom stood on the balcony of his bedroom. Mahir came and stood next to him. "Are you ready to go?" he asked. "Well, I'm packed," said Tom, "but I'm not sure I'm ready to leave the Kingdom. By the way, has your father decided what to do with that journalist, Jake, yet?"

"Well, as you know, Jake has apologized[2] to my father. He actually loves our Kingdom and he and my father get on really well. I think he really is sorry for what he did. My father has forgiven[3] him in his heart. But of course he must be punished for what he did. He'll stay here in the palace prison for a year."

1　reward [rɪˋwɔrd] (v.) 報答；獎賞
2　apologize [əˋpɑləˌdʒaɪz] (v.) 道歉
3　forgive [fɚˋgɪv] (v.) 原諒（動詞三
　　態：forgive; forgave; forgiven）

4　fair [fɛr] (a.) 公正的
5　let off 寬恕

"That sounds fair[4]," said Tom. "After all, he nearly killed us. I was worried your father would let him off[5] completely."

"No, he wouldn't do that. He's not used to punishing people and it's not an easy thing for him to do. But I think he was quite frightened by what happened."

"Yeah, I think we had a very lucky escape," said Tom. "Back at school, when I was packing, Cornelius said he might not see me again and he was nearly right!"

"Well, at least we've proved Cornelius wrong again," said Mahir and he looked at his watch. "Hey, we'd better get going or you'll miss your plane!"

An hour later, Mahir, Tara and Tom were sitting in the departure[1] lounge at the airport. Tom's flight to Kathmandu was leaving in fifteen minutes

"Have you enjoyed yourself?" asked Tara.

"I can honestly say that it was the most exciting holiday I've ever had!" said Tom.

"You haven't missed TV?"

"No, I haven't," said Tom, "I haven't had time. But there is one thing I'm looking forward to in England."

"What's that?" asked Mahir.

"A whopper hamburger and French fries," said Tom. "Without chili peppers," he added and they all laughed.

---

1 departure [dɪˋpɑrtʃɚ] (n.) 離開

AFTER READING

Ⓐ Characters

1 The adjectives describing the characters below are not the correct ones. Replace them with their opposites in the box.

wise
brave
strong
calm
fair
friendly
kind
adventurous

FALSE	TRUE
excitable	
weak	

FALSE	TRUE
unadventurous	
unkind	

FALSE	TRUE
unfriendly	
cowardly	

FALSE	TRUE
foolish	
unfair	

2 Which is your favorite character? Fill in a fact file for him/her.

Name
Age
Nationality
Hair color
Interests
Likes
Dislikes
Good at

3 Write the names of the characters beside the sentences.

_____ a He is English and he goes to a boys' boarding school in the south of England.

_____ b He stayed in a monastery for seven years and he learnt to be strong and brave.

_____ c She was the youngest competitor in the archery competition that year.

_____ d She was wise and brave and she was rescued by a snow leopard.

_____ e He is an American journalist and he lost his job.

_____ f They symbolize the peace and happiness of their country.

4 Listen and number the pictures.

a   b   c   d

5 Imagine you are a journalist. What questions would you ask the King? Ask and answer with a partner.

❸ Plot and Theme

6 Answer the questions.

- ⓐ What is the small light flashing at the school gate?
- ⓑ What does Cornelius think will happen to Tom in the Kingdom of the Snow Leopard?
- ⓒ Which mountain do they see on their flight to the Kingdom of the Snow Leopard?
- ⓓ What does Tom think will happen during the flight?
- ⓔ What are the three masks that Tara makes?
- ⓕ Why is Mahir upset during the archery competition?
- ⓖ Why does Jake kidnap Tom, Tara and Mahir?
- ⓗ What does Jake think the Shining Star is?
- ⓘ Why are Tom and Tara lucky at the end of the story?
- ⓙ What will Tom eat when he gets back to England?

7 With a partner find the things in the text which symbolize the words below.

- ⓐ Life
- ⓑ Strength and courage
- ⓒ Peace and happiness
- ⓓ Wisdom
- ⓔ Friendship
- ⓕ Freedom
- ⓖ Truth
- ⓗ Peace and tranquility

8 Read the text about Jake and choose the best word for each space.

Jake is an American journalist and he lives in America. He is very interested (a) _____ the Kingdom of the Snow Leopard and he knows a lot about the history and (b) _____ of the country. One day, he loses his job and he doesn't have any (c) _____ . A rich man called Jack Sharpe contacts Jake. He asks him to (d) _____ the Shining Star from the King of the Kingdom of the Snow Leopard. In return, he will give Jake a lot of money. Jake (e) _____ .

Jake goes to the Kingdom and he (f) _____ Tom, Tara and Mahir. Mahir takes him to the Temple of the Moon where the Shining Star is. Jake is very (g) _____ when he finally sees the Shining Star. He regrets his evil acts. The King (h) _____ him but the punishment is not very harsh.

_____ ⓐ ① in　　② at　　③ for

_____ ⓑ ① life　　② entertainment　　③ politics

_____ ⓒ ① wealth　　② money　　③ hope

_____ ⓓ ① attack　　② destroy　　③ steal

_____ ⓔ ① agrees　　② refuses　　③ smiles

_____ ⓕ ① kidnaps　　② meets　　③ makes friends with

_____ ⓖ ① happy　　② disappointed　　③ jealous

_____ ⓗ ① punishes　　② congratulates　　③ thanks

9 What differences does Tom find between England and the Kingdom of the Snow Leopard? With a partner write a list. Then discuss as a class.

C Language

10 Match the following expressions with their meanings.

_____ a I'll take your word for it.   1 I'm very hungry.
_____ b A shiver ran down my spine.   2 That's good.
_____ c Wicked.   3 I should leave now.
_____ d I'd better get going.   4 I suddenly felt afraid.
_____ e I'm starving.   5 I believe you.

Practice the Present Perfect with Yet, Already and Just

11 Complete the short dialogues with yet, already or just.

1 Mahir

Have you finished packing _____?

No, I haven't finished _____.

Tom

Mahir

Have you made the masks _____?

2

Yes, I've _____ made them. They are hanging in your bedroom.

Tara

90

Tara

Have you had breakfast
_____?

3

Yes, we have _____
finished it. It was very hot
and spicy.

Tom

Tom

4

Where's Tara?

I've _____ seen
her. She's in the garden.
She's practicing for the
archery competition.

Mahir

Practice Have To/Don't Have To

12 Complete the sentences with the correct form of have to or
don't have to.

a Tom and Mahir .... stay in Britain during the school holidays.

b Tom .... have a visa to travel to the Kingdom of the Snow
Leopard.

c Tom and Mahir .... wear traditional clothes in the Kingdom
of the Snow Leopard.

d They .... fly by Dragon Air to the Kingdom of the Snow
Leopard because no other airline flies there.

Practice Make and Let

13 Complete the sentences with the correct form of make or let.

[a] The King .... Tara enter the archery competition.

[b] Mahir .... Tom ride on the back of his horse.

[c] He doesn't .... him ride another horse.

[d] Jake .... Tom sit on the ground next to Tara.

[e] Jake .... Mahir take him to the Shining Star.

Practice the Present and Past Passive

14 Complete the sentences with the Present or Past Passive form of the verbs in brackets.

[a] A lot of chili .... (eat) in the Kingdom of the Snow Leopard.

[b] Traditional dress .... (wear) in the Kingdom of the Snow Leopard.

[c] Tom and Mahir .... (greet) by the King and Queen at the airport.

[d] The masks .... (make) by Tara.

[e] Princess Kia .... (rescue) by a snow leopard.

[f] Tara, Tom and Mahir .... (kidnap) by Jake.

[g] Jake .... (take) to the Temple of the Moon by Mahir.

[h] Jake .... (punish) by the King.

1 Complete the information for a tourist brochure about the
Kingdom of the Snow Leopard. You will find the information
you need in the story.

THE KINGDOM OF THE SNOW LEOPARD

The Kingdom of the Snow Leopard is a magical place. It is in the
[1] _____ Mountains. It is a quiet, peaceful place. There are no
[2] _____ there so people travel around on [3] _____ or on
[4] _____ .

FOOD
The food is very [5] _____ and there are _ [6] _____ in everything.
Vegetables are an important part of the diet and many people are
[7] _____ . However some people do eat meat, usually [8] _____
meat.

SPORTS
The national sport is [9] _____ and there is an important [10]
_____ held every year. Martial arts are also very popular. Men and
[11] _____ compete together in all sporting events.

VISAS
You [12] _____ have a visa to go to the Kingdom of the Snow
Leopard. It is best to apply for your visa early because only [13] _____
tourists can visit the country each year.

We wish you a peaceful and pleasant stay in our country.

2 Tom is going to a country he has never been to before. Which country would you like to visit for the first time? Find out about it on the Internet. Use the model on page 94 to create a tourist brochure for it.

3 Tara tells Tom the legend of Princess Kia and the snow leopard. Choose a myth or legend from your country and write a short paragraph about it.

4 Read the short text about masks in Bhutan and choose the correct word for each space.

MASKS IN BHUTAN

Masks play a/an (a)............ part in the story. They also play an important part in the lives of the people of Bhutan. In Bhutan masked dances are a common form of (b)............ for the people during festivals known (c)............ Tshechus. Each dance has its (d)........... special meaning. The dances are (e)............ in monasteries and have special religious significance.

a	① important	② weird	③ equal
b	① work	② entertainment	③ life
c	① of	② for	③ as
d	① own	② self	③ their
e	① perform	② performing	③ performed

5 Is there an occasion or festival in your country when people wear masks? What do the different masks symbolize? Do you know? Write a short paragraph and illustrate it.

那個人沒有作聲，旋即掉頭逃走。那個傢伙長得高高瘦瘦的，禿頭，眼睛是棕色的，長相沒有特別的特徵，但他臉上有一道長長的疤痕，從左眼角往下一直劃到嘴角。

「你想他為什麼要偷拍你？」湯姆問。

P.13

「我不知道。」馬希爾回答。

「如果他是個危險分子，怎麼辦？我覺得我們應該去跟老師報告。」

「不用了，我不想這麼做。」馬希爾立刻回答。

「既然這樣，那我覺得你應該告訴你爸才對。」湯姆憂心地說。

「不行，這樣只會讓他擔心，然後派更多的保鏢給我，我可不想這樣。」馬希爾說。

「可是你不怕嗎？那傢伙搞不好是個殺手，要來殺你的。」湯姆說道。

「噢，是嗎？我看你是驚悚片看太多了。」馬希爾說。

「我可以保護自己，這你知道的，湯姆。」

馬希爾接著挽住了湯姆的臂膀，然後迅雷不及掩耳地來個過肩摔，把湯姆給摔倒在地上。

「好好好，我知道，你可以保護自己，這招過肩摔很完美，一點也不會傷到人。」湯姆說。

「我們是不可以傷到對手的，只要制止就行了，這是我們國家的格鬥規則。現在，站起來吧。」馬希爾說。

「你也知道，我站不起來。」湯姆說。

他無法移動自己的手臂或腳，他的手腳變得很沉重，甚至連一根手指都動不了，實在很不可思議！馬希爾慢慢踱步走向湯姆，把手放在他肩上，用大姆指壓了一下，「現在，可以起來了。」他平靜地說道，而湯姆果然站了起來。

「你是怎麼辦到的？」湯姆問。

「常練習就可以了，記住，『熟能生巧』，現在換你試試看。」馬希爾說。

P.14

力量

• 你有練過什麼武術嗎？你對下列的武術有何了解？這些武術各自發展出了什麼樣的技巧？
a) 柔道　　b) 空手道　c) 合氣道
d) 太極拳　e) 跆拳道　f) 功夫

湯姆於是拎起馬希爾的手臂，並用手指頭壓住，然後使出一記過肩摔，把馬希爾摔到地上。馬希爾立刻站了起來，「這一記摔得不錯，不過你要運用你的專注力。」他說。

「這我做不來。」湯姆說。

「你一定可以的，你一直在進步中，」馬希爾冷靜地說：「只要你相信自己可以做得到，那你就一定可以做得到。我想晚餐時間到了，我們走吧。」

「好啊，我快餓死了，我們來看誰先跑到餐廳！」湯姆說。

不消說，當然是馬希爾贏了，只要是運動比賽，他都是第一名。他的體格很好，結實有力。湯姆回想起他們一起剛來學校的第一個星期，那年他們才都

十一歲，兩個人都很想家。在英國南部昂貴的寄宿學校裡生活著實不易，有一天晚上，兩人都睡不著，當時是九月初，晚上還滿暖和的，兩人於是一起躡手躡腳地溜出宿舍，來到外面的校園裡。他們沿著車道走，來到橡樹下的那張木椅上坐下，他們多年來的友誼就是從那時候開始的。

那個晚上，馬希爾跟湯姆說了一件事情，讓湯姆畢生難忘──這件事情講出了馬希爾一身氣力的祕密。

P.15

「在我四歲的時候，父王帶我到喜馬拉雅山的一間佛寺，那裡很高，沒有路可以到，只能靠著些小徑上山。當時大雪漫天紛飛，地上都結冰了，路很難走。後來我父親把我留在寺廟裡，和一位老僧待在一起。當我們第一次走進佛寺時，我很害怕。那些出家人當時正在誦經，聲音很大聲，空氣中香煙彌漫，而且有一種很香的奇特味道。我緊緊抓住我爸的手，把臉藏在他的長袍後面。接著，那位老僧踏著一條長長的紅地毯，向我走過來。他笑容可掬，看起來慈眉善目的。當他走到我身邊時，拉起了我的手握住，那好冷，但我感到很溫暖，而且不再害怕。從那天起，我就不曾再恐懼過。我在那位出家人的身邊待了七年，他教了我很多東西，他教會我控制自己的意志、征服恐懼，並且教我如何在沒有食物的情況下活下來、如何在冰天雪地中保持體溫，還有，他也教我如何在戰鬥中取勝卻不會傷到任何人。」

P.17

獨立

- 你第一次離家是在什麼時候？那次待在外面的時間有多久？你當時和誰在一起？
- 如果被送進寺廟裡住一年的話，你會懷念家裡的什麼東西？請列出一張表，和同伴分享。

「那你可以教我嗎？」湯姆問道。

馬希爾盯著他看了好一會兒，說道：「我想我們會是好朋友，所以我可以教你。」

這些是五年前的往事了，如今他們成了死黨，而馬希爾也教會了湯姆許多東西。

終於，來到學期的最後一天了，湯姆很興奮，爸媽再一個小時就會來接他和馬希爾，他難以置信他們就要啟程了。

他現在人在宿舍裡打包行李，這時寇

尼力走進來，一屁股坐在床上。寇尼力雖然很聰明、很有趣，但是卻也很沒品，湯姆不喜歡他。馬希爾剛到學校就讀的第一年，他老是喜歡嘲弄馬希爾，所以湯姆和馬希爾都盡量避免和他打照面。

「聽說你耶誕假期要和馬希爾去他那個怪胎國家，你一定是瘋了！」寇尼力說。

「那不是什麼怪胎國家，我就是想跟馬希爾去。」湯姆生氣地說道。

「你確定你要去一個沒有電視、沒有網路、沒有手機的地方？你會無聊死的。」寇尼力說。

「生命中還有比電視和網路更重要的東西。」湯姆說道。

「譬如？」寇尼力說。

「譬如到處遊歷，學習認識不同的文化，看看別人是如何生活的。」

「好棒噢！」寇尼力打著哈欠說道：「我呢，今年的耶誕節會和爸媽去瑞士滑雪，住在擁有最新科技設備的豪華飯店裡。」

「那就祝你玩得愉快。」湯姆說。

「那還用說！我想我下學期還會看到你吧，不過也很難講，搞不好那個怪胎國家的人會把你關起來，或是你會被喜馬拉雅山的雪人攻擊，最後客死異鄉。」寇尼力說。

「真是笑話，寇尼力。我現在要打包行李。」湯姆說。

寇尼力又待一會兒後才離開。

湯姆打包好之後，就去找馬希爾。「他去哪裡了？」他心想：「一整個上午都沒看到他，爸媽很快就要到了。」

馬希爾隨即就要去湯姆家過夜，當然，馬希爾的保鑣也會隨行，然後第二天大夥兒就要開拔到機場，一起前往雪豹王國。

湯姆得到國王特別的邀請，他覺得很榮幸。邀請函就放在他的口袋裡，那是一張白色的卡片，上面寫著紅色和金色的美麗藏文。

湯姆終於找到馬希爾了，他人就坐在長凳上，看著家長們開車進入校園。湯姆在他旁邊坐了下來，等待爸媽開車到來。「謝天謝地，學期終於結束了。」湯姆心想：「這個宿舍我連一個晚上都待不下去了，我只想再睡在自己的房間裡。」

「之後就聽不到上下課的鈴聲了。」馬希爾說道，打斷了湯姆的思緒。

「也吃不到一塊一塊的冷麥片粥早餐了。」湯姆說。

「也不用再考法文字彙了。」馬希爾說。

「不會再被邁爾斯先生處罰放學後不准離開教室了。」湯姆說。

「星期六早上不用繞著結冰的足球場跑步了。」馬希爾說。

「我還以為你喜歡運動。」湯姆說。

「我是喜歡啊，但不包括足球。我喜歡需要專注力或技巧的運動，像是柔道、空手道或是射箭。」馬希爾說。

這兩個男孩繼續接龍說著「不用再……」，直到湯姆父親的銀色車子駛進校門。

P. 20

　第二天早上，馬希爾穿上了傳統的衣服「幗」，那是一種長袍，腰際間綁了一條布帶，稱作「卡拉」。「幗」是由華麗的紅色和金色絲線織成，兩個袖子上還各繡了一隻紅眼金龍。

　「他現在看起來真是貴為王子了。」湯姆心想。

　湯姆此行沒有帶上太多東西，只準備了一些禮物要送給國王、王后、馬希爾的妹妹和四個弟弟。

　「你不需要帶太多衣服，進入我們的國家之後，就要換穿我們的傳統衣服。」馬希爾說。

P. 21

　他們先搭乘英國航空的飛機到尼泊爾的加德滿都，然後再轉機去雪豹王國。只有一個航線可以飛到王國，那是王國自營的龍航公司，每星期只有兩班飛機從加德滿都飛來，另外還有一班從曼谷飛來。

　下午三點左右，他們抵達加德滿都，有兩位從皇宮來的僧人在那裡等候迎接他們。兩位僧人先是鞠躬致敬，然後其

中一人向馬希爾說了些話，並交給他一個包裹。馬希爾向對方致謝，然後轉身對湯姆說：「這是你的衣服，你現在就換上，薩米爾會幫你穿。」

　其中一位僧人這時走向前來，向湯姆鞠了一躬，然後帶他進入貴賓休息室。那裡有淋浴間和更衣室，湯姆打開包裹，小心翼翼取出一件深藍色與金色相間的「幗」，僧人接著幫他穿上，並繫上卡拉。湯姆的個頭比雪豹王國的一般人來得高大，所以這些衣服都是為他量身訂做的。這一身藍色的長袍，把他的藍色眼珠烘托得更藍了。當他看著鏡中的自己時，自己都嚇了一跳，「現在我看起來也像個王子啦。」他心想。之後他走出休息室，來到馬希爾所待的頂級貴賓室。

P. 22

　然而就在他步入貴賓室時，卻看到了那個臉上有疤痕的男子，他不禁心跳加速，男子則把目光移開。

　「這個男人為什麼會在這裡？他為什麼要跟蹤馬希爾？」湯姆喃喃自問。他看著男子走進餐廳後，趕緊往貴賓室奔去。

　「怎麼啦？」馬希爾看到湯姆緊張的表情便問道。

　「那個臉上有疤的傢伙也在機場，就是上次在學校偷拍你的那個人。」湯姆用恐慌的語氣說道。

　「我知道，我在倫敦的機場就看到他了。」馬希爾說。

　「你怎麼沒告訴我？」湯姆說。

　「我不想嚇到你。那個人在監視我，

不過他傷不了我的。」馬希爾說。

「你不知道問題的嚴重性，他可以拿槍射殺你，可以置你於死地。」湯姆說。

「不會的，他不會這麼做。」馬希爾冷靜地說道：「既然他在英國沒有下手，那他在這裡就更不會下手了。他只是想從我這裡弄到什麼東西，只是我不知道那是什麼東西。我們只要靜觀其變，很快就會知道的。」

「你確定？」湯姆問道。

「我確定。」馬希爾嘴巴上這麼說，但心裡並沒有把握。

「這個男人到底要做怎樣？」馬希爾自問道：「他是想殺我，還是綁架我？他在英國時為什麼不動手？在英國下手要方便多了，要是皇宮，有好幾百個人守衛。雪豹王國是一個和平的國家，希望他不會把暴力帶進來。」

P.23

「嘿，馬希爾，他們已經在廣播了，走吧，要登機了。」湯姆說。

「走吧。」馬希爾向朋友笑了笑，說道：「你一定會愛死這趟飛行的。」

他們搭的是小飛機，只有三十五名乘客。

「真酷，我還沒坐過這麼小的飛機。」湯姆說。

「你很幸運，可以在白天飛這一趟，我們等一下可以看到聖母峰，飛越世界的最高峰。」馬希爾說。

「酷！那就不用辛苦地爬了。」湯姆說。

他們坐上椅子，繫好安全帶，這時湯姆抬起頭，看到那名臉上有疤的男子也上了飛機。

「我真不敢相信，那個傢伙也上了飛機，他也要去雪豹王國。」他說。

「別擔心，湯姆，他不會怎樣的。」馬希爾平靜地說。

「他要是劫持飛機怎麼辦？」湯姆問。

「不會的，他不會這麼做的。我跟你說了，他只是想要我國家裡的什麼東西。我們先別管他，好好享受這趟飛行吧。」馬希爾說。

P.24

飛機起飛了，湯姆看到喜馬拉雅山就在眼前。飛機愈飛愈高，升到了宏偉的山脈之上。飛機逐步往上爬升之際，湯姆屏住了呼吸，下面的群峰白雪皚皚，非常壯觀。

「我們很幸運，今天的天氣很好，不像有時候強風肆虐，飛機飛起來時驚心動魄的。」馬希爾說。

一個半小時之後，小飛機在雪豹王國著陸，湯姆終於鬆了一口氣。

「我們暫時算是平安了，那個臉上有疤的傢伙沒有劫機。」他心想。

「你看！」馬希爾邊說邊用手指向窗外，「我爸媽來接機了。」

湯姆朝窗外望去，看到小機場的大廈外面站了一些人。那是一些身穿橘色長袍的僧人，和一些穿著金、紅色相間的袍子的男人，在那群人的中間則是一對男女，分別坐在兩張椅子上。

「他們一定就是馬希爾的爸媽了。」湯姆心想。

飛機在一條長長的紅色地毯前著陸，當空服員打開飛機大門時，湯姆聽到了陣陣樂聲傳來，那種音樂很奇怪、也很震撼，聽起來有點像笛子的聲音。他們坐在那裡等待，直到其他的乘客都下了飛機。

僧人們遞給每個乘客一個由橘色花朵所做成的小手鐲。「他們拿給乘客的東西是什麼？」湯姆問道。

P.26

「那是橘色小花，是快樂的象徵，那些乘客都是我們的賓客，我們希望他們在我們的國家裡都是快快樂樂的。」馬希爾解釋道。

湯姆注意到那個疤面男子正沿著紅色的地毯快步而走，然後步入機場大廈裡。「或許我應該把這傢伙的事告訴馬希爾的爸爸。」湯姆心想。

當湯姆和馬希爾最後踏上紅地毯時，眾僧都鞠躬相迎，並且給湯姆和馬希爾每人各一個用橘色花朵做成的手鐲。接著，國王和王后站在地毯的末端，馬希爾先向父親鞠了一躬，然後又向母親行了同樣的禮，湯姆見狀也有樣學樣地照做。

P.27

「歡迎來到雪豹王國。」國王用英語說道。

「謝謝您，我很高興能夠來到貴國家。」湯姆說。

接著群僧穿過機場大廈，國王和王后跟在後面。第一次有朋友的父母以這種排場來歡迎湯姆，這種隆重的禮儀讓他感到尊榮，他很樂在其中。

機場大廈外面有一匹馬和一輛馬車在

103

待命著，國王和王后先上了車，馬希爾和湯姆隨後，之後馬車便啟程出發。

P.28

馬車沿著一條寬敞的馬路前進，兩側樹木夾道，路旁的民眾在他們經過時紛紛揮手致意，並且拋灑鮮花。

「這個國家的首都真是寧靜。」湯姆心想。不久，他明白了原因，因為這個國家的馬路上看不到汽車。

「這裡竟然連一輛車子都沒有！」他吃驚地說道。

「是沒有，汽車會造成污染，」國王說道：「而且車子充斥在城市的每個角落裡，會給人們的生活帶來很多壓力。這裡的人不是騎馬就是騎腳踏車，他們可以自由地在城裡到處走動，不會在車陣裡塞幾個小時無法動彈。」

「真酷。」湯姆說道。不過他無法想像他爸爸騎腳踏車上班的樣子，當然，他更無法想像媽媽騎著馬去採購。

這時，他們在馬路上轉了一個彎，湯姆看到眼前矗立了一座巍峨的山，在山坡高處有一棟用紅色、黑色和金色所漆成的建築物。

「那裡就是宮殿。」馬希爾說。

「哇，實在讓人大開眼界」湯姆說。

十分鐘後，馬車來到兩扇大木門的前面停了下來。宮殿的守衛把大門打開，等他們一行人通過之後，便又把門關起來。

「有人襲擊過皇宮嗎？」湯姆好奇地問。

「沒有。」國王回答：「沒有人襲擊過皇宮，我的人民沒有起義的理由，這裡的生活和平而幸福。而且，要襲擊皇宮並不是一件簡單的事，宮殿的守衛精通武術，沒有人能夠打過他們闖入宮殿裡。」國王這時直視著湯姆，說道：「為什麼你會這麼問呢？」

P.29

湯姆覺得自己臉紅了，他先看看馬希爾，然後目光又落回國王身上。他很想說「沒什麼」，可是他沒辦法向眼前這個人撒謊。「有一個人在跟蹤馬希爾。」他說完便把疤面男子的事告訴了國王。

「謝謝你跟我說這件事，」國王嚴肅地凝視著兒子，說道：「可是別擔心，馬希爾在這裡很安全。」

就在這時，馬車停了下來，只見宮殿樓梯跑下來一個女孩，往馬車這邊飛奔過來。她年約十五歲，身材很窈窕，有一頭烏黑亮麗、又直又長的頭髮，臉上的笑容很甜美，長得很漂亮。

「這是我妹妹。」馬希爾邊說邊跳出了馬車。

「你終於回來了，我真不敢相信。」女孩開心地說道，馬希爾給她一個大大的擁抱。

「快來見見湯姆。湯姆，這位是我妹妹多羅。」馬希爾說。

「嗨。」湯姆說。

「哈囉，湯姆，終於見到你了，太棒了！馬希爾跟我說了很多你的事，來吧，我現在帶你去看你的房間。明天是一個大日子，所以有很多事情要做，我已經幫你們做了一些面具，服裝也準備好了，不過你們要試穿一下。」多羅興奮地繼續說道。

P.30

「要記得,晚上八點在紅色餐廳用晚餐。」王后吩咐道。

一行人拾級而上,湯姆就跟在後面。他們穿過一條通道,來到一座長滿了橘色和黃色鮮花的中庭。

「這裡叫做『太陽中庭』。」馬希爾說:「在我們的王國裡,太陽是『幸福』的象徵,在走過這座中庭時,上天會賜福給你。」

接著他們又走進另一扇門,來到另一座中庭,這座中庭裡的花朵都是藍色的。

「這裡叫做『天空中庭』,在我們的王國裡,蔚藍的天空象徵著『和平寧靜』。在皇宮中一旦有人感到憤怒時,就會來這座中庭裡坐,讓怒氣消失,在離開這裡時,心裡就會感到平靜了。」多羅解釋道。

他們又穿過另一扇門,來到第三座中庭,這裡的鮮花都是白色的。

「這裡叫『白雪中庭』,在我們王國裡,白雪象徵『真理』,當你行經這座中庭時,上天便會提醒你真理的重要性。」馬希爾說:「在雪豹王國裡,我們最重視的價值是快樂、和平和真理。」

P.31

顏色

• 你最喜歡什麼顏色?它帶給你什麼樣的感覺?對你有什麼樣的象徵?和同伴一起討論。

• 請針對下面的每種顏色,寫出一個與之相符的形容詞。
  □ 白色　　□ 綠色　　□ 黑色
  □ 紅色　　□ 藍色　　□ 黃色

這時有兩位身穿橘色長袍的僧人打開他們面前的一扇金色大門,三位少年男女便走進了宮殿。湯姆原以為皇宮裡一定是富麗堂皇,但事實並非如此,裡面的牆面都是白色的,地板是石板鋪成的。他們往上走過幾個台階,來到一道長廊,在走廊底有兩扇門。

「這是你的房間。」多羅邊說邊打開第一扇門。

房間裡擺了一張很大的木床,鋪著橘色的床罩,上面擺放著好幾個橘色和金色的墊子。再推開另一扇門,則是一間鋪著白色瓷磚的浴室。另外還有兩扇門向外通向大陽台。從陽台上往外望去,是一片森林和山下的城市。湯姆站在陽台上,看到由紅色瓷磚所砌成的美麗屋頂,煙囪裡炊煙裊裊。他看到炊煙升空到樹林之上,然後消失在蔚藍的天空裡,他內心裡感到一種喜悅。

P.32

「快來。」馬希爾這時說道:「我帶你去看我的房間。」

馬希爾的房間比湯姆的大,但是看

起來不像是青少年的房間，白色的牆壁上看不到海報，書桌上也沒有電腦或電視，牆上只掛了三個木製的面具。

「那是什麼？」湯姆問。

「這是明天節慶要用的，是我幫我們三個人做的，我花了好幾天的時間才做好的，我想把它們做得特別不一樣，因為這是湯姆參加的第一個節慶。」多羅說。

多羅拿下第一個面具，那是一張金龍的臉，有一對紅色的大眼睛。

「馬希爾，這個面具當然是你的了。根據我們的傳統，只有國王的長子才能穿著龍服參加『金光節』。」她一邊把面具交給馬希爾，一邊跟湯姆解釋道。

P.33

接著她又取下第二個面具，「湯姆，這是給你的。」她邊說邊把面具遞給他。「這是雪豹，傳說中提到，雪豹曾經從生死的危難中把姬雅公主救出來。」

「姬雅公主是誰？」湯姆問道。

「她是我們的祖先，是一位智勇雙全的女性。」多羅說：「有一天，她聽說有一個農夫的犛牛被偷了，便決定前去找當地的行政官員解決這個問題。每個城堡都派駐有行政官員，官員就住在城堡裡，而這些城堡往往是蓋在崇山峻嶺的山頂。當姬雅公主策馬來到城堡時，正好下起雪來，紛飛的大雪讓她迷了路。這時她的騎的馬摔倒了，摔下馬背的公主在冰天雪地中失去了意識。公主在昏迷時做了一個夢，她夢到一隻孔武有力、全身毛皮潔白如雪的動物來到她身邊，把她馱到自己的背上，然後沿著

冰封的山路，把她載到城堡的大門邊放下。當她醒過來時，發現自己躺在城堡裡的床上，人們告訴她，她是在城堡的大門外面被發現，『原來是那隻雪豹救了我。』公主說。」

P.35

「雖然這只是一個傳說，但很多人都相信，善人遇難時，雪豹就跑來救他們，雪豹是力量和勇氣的象徵。」馬希爾說。

湯姆伸手接過這個白色面具，面具上有銀色豹斑和一雙翠綠色的眼睛。「多羅，很謝謝你，這做得很漂亮。」他說。

多羅接著拿下第三個面具，說道：「這是我的面具。」

這個面具是一個美麗女性的臉，眼睛也是翠綠色的。

「這個面具上畫的就是姬雅公主，希望明天晚上你不必出面來救我。」多羅

笑著說道。

不過多羅說這番話時，湯姆背脊發涼，打了一個冷顫。「明天晚上會有什麼不好的事發生，我可以感覺出來。」他心想。

「看看時間，快八點了，我們去吃晚餐吧。」馬希爾這時說道。

湯姆壓下不安的感覺，跟隨馬希爾和多羅走出房間。他們兄妹倆有說有笑，不久湯姆也跟著笑了起來。

晚餐的菜很辣，湯姆吃得滿頭大汗。「這個咖哩可真辣，吃得我第一次流這麼多的汗。」他說。

「我們國家的人常說：『如果不出汗，寧可不吃飯』，指的就是這種辣椒。不過我已經吩咐大廚在你的飯菜裡少放些辣椒了。」多羅說。

P.36

「你是說你的菜更辣？」湯姆吃驚地問。

「沒錯。」多羅說完便笑了起來。

「這比印度所有的辣椒都還要辣。」湯姆說。

接著他對著那張長長的木桌望過去，只見所有的僧侶、警衛和宮廷人員，都大汗淋漓地在那裡津津有味地吃著。

「這道菜很特別，是優格乳酪做成的。我們先把優格乳酪拿來加奶油、加糖一起炸過，然後再加入紅辣椒。」多羅說。

「這些食物都是辣的嗎？」

「沒錯，都是辣的，我們連早餐也是辣的，我們的粥就是用穀類、奶油、糖和辣椒煮成的。」

湯姆這時吃了一大匙的飯，「至少飯不是辣的。」他心想，於是又扒了一匙飯，然後喝了口飲料。

「這是酥油茶，我們在用餐時通常會喝酥油茶、葡萄酒或是米釀的啤酒。」多羅說。

酥油茶很甜，喝起來有焦糖的味道，很對湯姆的味。「這裡的人吃肉嗎？」他問。

「有些人會吃肉，吃犛牛的肉，不過我們國家大部分的人都吃素，我們宮殿裡也不太吃肉，只有在外賓來訪或是特殊的場合裡才會吃肉。我們不喜歡為了食物而屠殺動物。」多羅說。

就在這個時候，國王站了起來，發表談話。國王說道：「現在，我有一件特別的事情要宣布，射箭比賽在明天早上八點鐘開始進行，今年，我的女兒多羅也會出賽。」

P.37

多羅興奮得倒抽了一口氣，她站起身，微微地向大家鞠了一躬。父王朝她笑了笑，每個人在這時也都鼓起掌來。

「祝你旗開得勝。」國王說道。

「謝謝您，父親。」她說完後就坐了下來，說道：「真不敢相信，我這麼小，他們居然會讓我參加比賽。」

「參加什麼比賽？」湯姆問。

「明天上午的箭術比賽，這是一項很重要的比賽，來自全國各地的好手都會上場一較高下。我跟你過的，箭術是我們全國性的運動項目。」馬希爾說。

「是的，我知道，我們學校每年的射箭比賽都是你拿冠軍，別人根本射不贏你。」湯姆説。

「我也沒辦法呀，你們得多多練習才可以。」馬希爾説。

比賽

- 男性和女性應該一起比賽嗎？哪一種運動比賽可以不分性別？就以下的運動來討論：

  a) 足球　b) 武術　c) 賽跑　d) 溜冰
  e) 滑雪　f) 游泳　g) 舉重　h) 角力

P.38

「為什麼多羅對明天的比賽這麼興奮？」

「她是最年輕的選手，而且這是她第一次參加規模這麼大的比賽。在我們這裡，男性和女性是一同參賽的，男女不會分開來比賽。」馬希爾説。

「真的嗎？真是帥呆了。嘿，那你呢？你明天會參加比賽嗎？」湯姆説。

「當然會啊。」馬希爾説。

「既然這樣，那她就一點希望都沒有啦。」

「這可不一定，明天就等著看，她射箭很厲害的。」馬希爾説。

這時國王又宣布了其他的事，他説：「明天的節慶活動在晚上七點鐘開始，射箭比賽一結束，每個人就要做好準備，我們在『太陽中庭』集合，一點鐘出發。現在，祝大家今晚有個好眠，明天是又長又忙碌的一天。」國王説完後俯首致意，這時王后也站起來鞠了一個躬，接著每個人都紛紛站起來鞠躬回禮，國王和王后隨之離席。

馬希爾跟湯姆説明了各種細節。

「我們為什麼要那麼早就出發？」湯姆問道。

「節慶活動是在雪堡舉行，雪堡位在高山上，走去那裡要很久，而且路很不好走。」馬希爾説。

「那我們要怎麼去？」湯姆問。

P.39

「騎馬呀。」馬希爾回答。

「你在開玩笑吧，我根本沒騎過馬！」湯姆滿面愁容地説。

「別擔心，你坐我的馬。」馬希爾説。

「我太興奮了，晚上一定會失眠的。」多羅説。

「我呢，可累了，應該要上床睡覺了。」湯姆説。

「我也睏了，我們折騰了一整天。」馬希爾説。

第二天早上，湯姆起了個大早。他走出房間，來到陽台上，看到多羅正在下面的花園裡，手裡還拎著弓和箭。湯姆看著她好一會兒，她謹慎地瞄靶發矢，只見箭咻咻凌空而過，射向一百公尺外的一棵大樹，直接命中樹上一個小小的紅色靶子。

「哇，她好厲害！」湯姆心想。

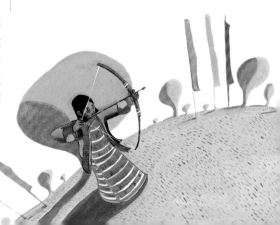

P.40

就在這時，多羅抬頭看到了湯姆，對他笑了笑，並揮了揮手，湯姆也向她揮手致意。

接著，傳來了敲門聲。湯姆把門打開，看到馬希爾就站在門口。馬希爾穿著一件黃色和金色相間的長幗，手裡拿著一個中世紀款式的頭盔和弓箭。

「你這樣看起來好像中世紀的騎士。」湯姆說。

「這跟我們學校的運動裝備很不一樣，對吧？」馬希爾笑著說道：「拿著，讓你看看頭盔有多重。學校的運動裝備是好多了。」

湯姆於是接過金色的頭盔。「是很重！」湯姆邊說邊試戴，「我這模樣看起來如何？」

「這和牛仔褲不太搭。」馬希爾說。

「是不太搭沒錯，說到牛仔褲，你可以幫我換上長幗嗎？我自己不會穿。」

「你要自己學會穿，我總不能每天都來幫你穿衣服吧。」馬希爾說。

這天早上的早餐是在一個小房間裡吃，只有湯姆和馬希爾兩個人而已。他們圍著一張矮桌子，席地坐在墊子上。一位僧人端來一個圓形大托盤，上面有一大碗加了辣椒的麥片粥、一些雜糧麵包和酥油茶。

「大家都去哪裡了？」湯姆問。

「他們都吃過了，在皇宮裡都是在日出時就吃早餐的。」馬希爾說。

「你昨天晚上怎麼沒先告訴我？」湯姆說。

「我知道你不習慣早起，你在學校裡沒這麼早起過。」馬希爾說。

P.41

「這裡和學校不一樣。」湯姆說完，吃了一小匙的麥片粥。「噢，這不太辣嘛⋯⋯哇！」這時辣椒嗆得他舌頭和喉嚨直發麻。「我的嘴巴裡著火了。」湯姆邊說邊連忙啃了一大塊的雜糧麵包，「我想我一定吃不慣這麼辣的食物。」

「你會習慣的，等到假期結束時，你就會覺得一點也不辣。等你回英國後，你會在漢堡裡猛放辣椒。」馬希爾說。

這時門被打開，多羅走了進來，「快點。兩位。」她說：「典禮再十分鐘就要開始了。」她穿了一件紫色和金色相間的「旗拉」，拿著一頂金色頭盔和弓箭。

「你吃飽了嗎？」馬希爾問湯姆。

「吃飽了，吃得很脹。」湯姆說道。

「那我們就走吧。」馬希爾說。

馬希爾領著他們穿過一條宛如迷宮的長廊，來到宮殿的後面。最後，他們來到了一個大房間，裡面擠滿了人。

「出賽的選手要在這個房間裡等候，你可以和我的弟弟們一起去逛逛，也可以和我的其他家人坐在棚子裡，我和多羅要待在這裡。」馬希爾說。

馬希爾於是帶著湯姆來到幾位弟弟站立的地方，「湯姆要過來和你們坐在一起。」他說完便跟他們介紹了湯姆。

P.42

馬希爾是長子，他最小的弟弟薩米才六歲。薩米走過來握著湯姆的手說：「你可以坐在我旁邊。」

薩米説完便領著湯姆來到外頭。外面是一大片草原，其中三面都用青草舖成了階梯，階梯上有色彩鮮艷的墊子，人們就坐在墊子上面。他走到草地遠遠的另一頭，國王和王后就坐在那邊棚子的椅子上。

國王和王后站起身向湯姆躬身作禮，湯姆連忙鞠躬答禮。

「你就和我坐在一起吧，」國王説完便用手指了指他旁邊的那張椅子，湯姆於是走上前入座，而薩米就坐到他媽媽椅子旁邊的一個墊子上。

「湯姆，如果你又看到那個臉上有疤的男人，請告訴我。」國王説。

「當然，我一定會告訴你。」湯姆説。

「馬希爾是不會告訴我的，他認為他可以保護自己。」國王用英語冷靜地説道：「我已經查出那個人了，他是一名記者，住在美國，沒有犯罪記錄，但他有可能是個危險分子。他在報刊雜誌發表了很多我們王國的報導，他知道我們國家的很多事情。」這時，國王的聲音突然變得嚴肅起來，「湯姆，馬希爾的性命可能受到威脅，如果那個傢伙再接近我兒子的話，你一定要告訴我。」

「是的，陛下，我一定會告訴你。」湯姆回答。

P.43

這時，突然傳來一陣響徹雲霄的鐃鈸聲。

「噢，我想比賽就要開始了。」國王説道。

接著又是一陣鏗鏗鏘鏘的鐃鈸聲，參加比賽的選手走出房間，來到了廣場。

只見每個人都鼓起掌，參賽選手隨著鼓聲前進，來到王室的棚子前便停下腳步，向國王和王后鞠躬致意。

國王接著起身俯首答禮，説道：「現在比賽開始！」

接著群眾一陣歡呼，而參賽選手就端坐在王室棚子兩側的長椅子上。

這時，大會叫了前兩位選手的名字，兩位選手便走到廣場上，那裡立了兩個靶子，靶子上畫了三條龍：一條藍眼睛的黑龍，一條金眼睛的紅龍，和一條紅眼睛的金龍。

參賽選手必須先射中紅龍的金眼，然後再射金龍的紅眼，而如果射到黑龍的藍眼，就會帶來厄運。每位選手可以射兩箭，在射出第一箭之後，會有兩個人跑過去核對得分，然後跑回來把箭歸還給選手。

只見許多參賽選手都射中了紅龍的金眼，但始終沒有人射中紅眼。

P. 45

接著輪到多羅出場。她信心十足地步入廣場，然後射出第一箭，結果正中紅龍的金眼，群眾立刻爆出一陣歡呼。接著，她射出第二箭，命中了金龍的紅眼。

她收起箭，轉身向國王鞠躬致意，群眾的歡呼聲不絕於耳。

接下來輪到馬希爾了。他走進場中時，向湯姆揮了一下手，表情很鎮定，充滿了自信。

他第一箭正中紅龍的金眼，群眾響起了一陣歡呼，樂隊的鼓聲敲得震天價響。接著他又射出第二箭，只見群眾那裡傳來一陣焦急的耳語聲，然後一片鴉雀無聲，大家都一動也不動，也沒有人開口說話。

「馬希爾射中了黑龍的藍眼。」湯姆心想。

湯姆轉頭看了看國王，只見國王面色慘白，雙手緊緊抓住椅子的扶手。

馬希爾仍站在場上，他注視著靶子。多羅這時奔進場子，拉住哥哥的手，把他帶離廣場。

「馬希爾以前都沒有射中過藍眼。」國王說。

「如果他以前都沒射中過藍眼，為什麼今天會這樣？」湯姆很納悶，他不想再看接下來的比賽，只想去找馬希爾說話，可是他一定要等到比賽結束後才可以離席。

P. 46

最後，比賽終於結束了，他們宣布冠軍者是多羅公主。多羅走上棚子，從父親手中接過一個小金龍的雕像，然後面向觀眾舉起雕像。群眾響起如雷的歡呼聲，向公主鼓掌叫好。湯姆可以看出來，公主很受到歡迎。

其他的獎項紛紛頒出，接著多羅率領參賽選手走出廣場，國王、王后和皇室其他的成員們也跟在選手們之後離開，其他人則依舊坐在原地。

湯姆四處張望找馬希爾，但都沒有看到他。多羅向他走過時，湯姆問道：「馬希爾去哪去了？怎麼不在這裡？他還好嗎？」

「別擔心，我知道他在哪裡。」多羅說。接著多羅便帶著湯姆來到一座四周建有圍牆的小花園，馬希爾這時就坐在橘子樹下的草地上。

「他心情不好時，就會來這裡。」多羅小聲說道。

湯姆可以明白原因，因為這座花園很寧靜祥和。湯姆和多羅在馬希爾旁邊的草地上坐下來，三個人靜靜地坐了一會兒。

這時馬希爾說：「多羅，恭喜你，我以你為榮。」說完還給了她一個大大的擁抱。

「你是我的老師，我每樣東西都是從你那裡學來的。」多羅回答。

「謝了，現在你和湯姆應該準備去參加節慶活動。」馬希爾說。

「你不來嗎？」多羅有點沮喪地問。

「我不去，我想一個人靜一會兒。」馬希爾說。

就在這時，國王也走進了花園。「多羅，你和湯姆去換衣服，我要和兒子談談。」

P.47

困擾

• 你在心情沮喪時，通常都會找誰談？
  a) 父母 b) 朋友 c) 老師
• 你會和誰談哪方面的困擾？
  a) 老師 b) 母親 c) 父親 d) 朋友
• 和夥伴一起分享。

多羅緊緊握了一下哥哥的手，然後站起身來，湯姆也站了起來。他們走出花園時，湯姆問道：「國王生氣了嗎？」

「沒有，他從來都不生氣的。」多羅笑了一下說：「他是要和馬希爾聊，他會勸他今天下午和我們一起去參加節慶的。」

回到自己房間後，湯姆拿起他的面具，研究了一下。他用手指輕輕拂過這件精雕細琢的木製面具，摸著面具上漂亮的翠綠色眼睛，「雪豹到底是長得什麼樣子的？」

他想到雪豹的體力和腳力，想像牠輕巧躍過雪地的樣子。接著他把面具往臉上一戴，在鏡中端詳起來。

P.48

「這個面具有一股魔力，我可以感覺出來。」他心想，接著突然感到一股強烈的能量灌進自己的血液裡。

「這個面具讓我覺得自己變得很強壯。」他想，然後往空中做了一個跳躍。他覺得雙腿變得強而有力，可以輕鬆地跳躍。於是他這裡蹦蹦、那裡跳跳，而且跳得一次比一次高。

「真希望馬希爾也在這裡，」他想：「這樣他就可以跟我解釋這到底是怎麼回事了。」

這時，他感到有人走進房間，便向門轉身過去，只見門口站了一個人。湯姆看到那個人的臉上戴了金龍面具。

「馬希爾，你來了，你改變心意了。」湯姆開心地說。

「是的，」馬希爾拿下面具，說道：「爸爸跟我說了一件事，我心情好多了。」

「是什麼事？」湯姆一邊問，一邊拿下雪豹面具。

「在很多年前，我爸爸也參加了射箭比賽，那是他生平第一次的比賽。」

「你該不會是要告訴我，」湯姆插話道：「他也射中了藍眼睛了吧？」

P.49

「沒錯，他也射中了藍眼睛，而且他也和我一樣，感到很難過。」馬希爾說：「比賽結束後，他的父親也找他談，告訴他凡事只要往正面想，厄運自然就會遠離。他接受父親的教誨，結果什麼壞事情都沒發生。後來有一天，他騎馬上山時遇到暴風雪，在狂風暴雪中他什麼都看不見，不久便迷路了。他知道自己一定要在天黑之前找到路回家，不然在雪地裡待一整晚會沒命的。這時他在雪地上看到一小片橘色的衣服，於是連忙下馬，開始徒手在那小片衣服的四周挖起雪來，後來挖出了一位僧人的身體。所幸僧人一息尚存，我父親於是將僧人馱在馬背上，他現在知道附近一定有城堡，因為僧人不會穿這麼單薄的橘色長袍出門太遠的。一個小時之後，他果然找到了城堡。」

「那個僧人有活下來嗎？」湯姆問道。

「有，他活下來了。」馬希爾説：「僧人後來到皇宮裡和父親住，他們兩個人現在是很好的朋友。父親説，他的厄運，卻成了僧人的好運。他在大雪中迷路，卻救了僧人一命。我父親説，就算是厄運，也可以為別人帶來好運，而且好運的力量一定會勝過厄運。」

P.50

「希望如此。」湯姆説。

馬希爾接著説道：「現在趕快換好衣服吧，不然我們的厄運就是會錯過節慶活動。」

馬希爾從衣櫃裡拿出那件銀色和白色相間的長幗，幫湯姆穿上。

之後當馬希爾和湯姆來到太陽中庭時，大家都已經集合好了，只見什麼面具都有，像是老虎、馬匹、紅黑龍、勇士和魔王等。

「你們遲到啦。」一個聲音從湯姆身後傳來，他轉過頭去，看到了多羅。

多羅穿了一件銀色的旗拉，上面裝飾了用珠子串成的藍色小花，她的一頭又黑又長的秀髮從背後傾瀉而下，頭髮上還別著銀色小珠串，在陽光下閃閃發亮著。她的手上拿著自己的面具，看起來很俏麗。

「你會來救我嗎？」多羅開玩笑地問。

「當然啦。」湯姆回答。

「不管什麼危險都會？」她又問道。

「不管什麼危險都會！」湯姆説。

「你保證？」

「沒錯，我保證。」湯姆説。

這時，傳來了一陣鏗鏗鏘鏘的鐃鈸聲響，國王和王后正騎著馬跨過門，馬希爾緊跟在他們後面。馬希爾騎著一匹雄偉的黑馬，策馬來到湯姆面前，「你準備好了嗎？」他問完後便縱身跳下馬。

P.52

湯姆覺得根本無從準備起，他不會騎馬，並不想坐上馬。

馬希爾幫助他爬上馬鞍，然後自己縱身一躍也跳上馬。他們把面具放在一個袋子裡，然後掛在馬鞍上。接著馬希爾用腳後跟微微踢了一下馬，他們便策馬快步騎出中庭，來到長長的車道上。

湯姆緊緊靠在馬背上，雙眼緊閉，不過沒過多久，他就習慣了馬兒的奔跑，開始喜歡上了馬匹奔跑的速度。

「我還沒有騎馬走這麼遠的路過。」馬希爾在風中喊叫道：「在上山時就要把速度放慢，但我們現在可以和風賽跑。」沒錯，此刻的感覺正是和風賽跑。

他們風馳疾奔，湯姆回頭往後看，看到皇室的馬隊遠遠被拋在後面。

P.53

接著他看到一匹白色的雄馬快步地奔來，湯姆知道那一定是多羅。多羅的樣子看起來很英勇，無所畏懼。

「要我救她？應該是她來救我才對吧！」湯姆心想。

當他們開始上陡坡時，馬兒放慢了速度。前面的路愈來愈窄，到最後變成了一條小徑。

「現在，我總算知道這裡為什麼沒有汽車了，」湯姆心想：「根本就沒地方開嘛，根本就沒有又大又平的高速公路可以開大車奔馳。」他不知道馬希爾是否會懷念汽車，於是問道：「你不會懷念車子嗎？」

P.54

「為什麼要懷念車子？在英國，不是陷在車陣裡吸著排氣管所排出的漫天廢氣，就是時速只能開三十英哩，以免被超速照相機拍到，只要被照到三次，就會吊銷執照，那以後就只能搭公車啦。

所以你的好意我心領啦，我比較喜歡這裡，這裡不會塞車，而且想要騎多快就可以騎多快。」

「所以，如果你爸爸送你一輛紅色法拉利給當你十八歲的生日禮物，你會把禮物退還回去囉？」湯姆說。

馬希爾靜默了片刻，然後笑了起來，「我爸是不可能送我法拉利當作十八歲的生日禮物，不過如果他真的送了，我會是世界上最快樂的男孩。」

這時，他們轉進小徑的一個拐彎處，「不要往下看。」馬希爾大聲叫道。

當然，湯姆於是不由自主地往下看，底下是深不見底的峽谷，他看得很害怕。湯姆覺得腎上腺素急速上升，就像他第一次坐雲霄飛車那樣。「要是掉下去的話，會很久才著地。希望這些馬知道自己正在做什麼！」他說。

「不要擔心，這裡我來過幾百次啦。」馬希爾說。

湯姆望著前方白雪皚皚的群峰峰頂，「我們現在的位置很高了，對不對？」他說。

P.55

「其實還不算太高。我們現在離海拔三千公尺，還要爬一千公尺高才會到達城堡。」馬希爾回答。

「我第一次爬到這麼高的地方。」湯姆吃驚地說。

「哈囉！」多羅喊道，她的回音在群山之間迴盪著，她趕上了他們。

「現在已經離目的地不遠了。」馬希爾大聲地叫了回去。

接著他們又轉了一個拐彎處，湯姆終於看到了城堡。城堡就在下一座山的山側，「我們要去的地方就是那裡嗎？」他問

「是的，氣勢很驚人，對吧？」馬希爾說。

「我們要怎樣進去？城堡蓋在山崖邊吔！」湯姆問。

「到了那裡之後，你就會知道的。」馬希爾說。

P.56

他們又騎了兩個小時，城堡雖然一直在視線之內，卻好像可望而不可及。這時，狹窄的小徑突然出現了一個險峻的急彎，當他們小心翼翼地轉過去之後，竟變成了一條寬敞的路面——雖然不能和高速公路相提並論，但比起羊腸小徑是寬闊多了。

城堡的大木門就矗立在眼前，大門兩側各有一個人騎馬立在那裡，而且全身從頭到腳都是金色的打扮。大門是敞開的，湯姆瞄到裡面一片色彩繽紛。節慶已經開始，他聽到了鼓和笛子所傳來的陣陣聲響。

當他們下馬時，湯姆感到很興奮和激動。接著有兩個人走上前來，把他們的馬匹牽走。多羅、湯姆和馬希爾於是把面具戴上，踏著厚石板拱道，進入另一頭的中庭。

這不是搖滾演唱會，但卻一樣很刺激，他看到每個人都戴著面具上陣，連穿著橘色長袍的僧人也不例外。有老虎面具，面具上畫著黑色和橘色斑紋，立著小小的尖耳朵，瞪著一對綠色的大眼睛，還有猴子、馬和鳥等面具。

「每一種動物都代表不同的意義，老虎象徵力量，猴子象徵智慧，鳥象徵自由，馬象徵友誼。」多羅說。

P.57

「在你們的文化裡，你們認為動物是次等生命。你們雖然會愛護動物，卻不認為人類可以向動物學習。在我們這裡，我們很尊重動物，因為我們知道動物要比人類更具有力量。」馬希爾說。

「這話怎講？」湯姆問道。

「動物懂得傾聽大自然，牠們可以感覺到人類所感覺不到的東西，知道什麼時候會有暴風雨或地震，這我們人類就感受不到。」

這時，又傳來一陣鐃鈸聲，每個人都停下腳步，面向拱道。

「國王和王后到啦。」多羅小聲說道。

只見國王和王后步入拱道，每個人都紛紛鞠躬致敬，而國王和王后並沒有戴上面具。

「他們為什麼不戴面具？」湯姆問。

「因為他們就代表著自己的身分，國王和王后象徵一個國家的和平和快樂。」多羅說。

國王和王后坐在中庭另一邊的一個高高的平台上。兩人一座上王位，便響起一陣金屬與金屬互相撞擊所發出的鏗鏘聲，湯姆轉頭看到了一群戰士走進城堡，然後大步邁向中庭的中央。

P.58

動物

• 你的國家是如何對待動物的？你們認為動物是一種特別的生命嗎？
• 有任何和動物有關的傳說？請和同伴討論。

群眾紛紛安靜地讓出路。

「今晚的第一場舞蹈是刀劍之舞，這些是我們國家最優秀的軍人，每天都得操練五、六個小時。」馬希爾說。

「你好像說過，你們國家的人是不會拿武器作戰的。」湯姆說。

「的確不會，但我們的戰士個個劍術精湛。劍術是一種藝術，需要技巧和專注力。」馬希爾說。

人們在觀賞這些軍人的精彩表演時，太陽逐漸西沉，粉紅色天空逐漸黯淡，接著黑幕低垂。這時僧人們把城堡四面牆上的燈籠點亮，紅通通的燈籠不時明滅不定的閃爍著，光影投照在黑漆漆的中庭裡，面具上的大眼睛也被燭光烘托得更嚇人。

湯姆轉身想和多羅說說話，卻沒看到多羅。他環顧四周，都沒有看到她的人。

P.59

接著，他在石板地上看到了一塊金屬。他擠過人群，彎下身撿起金屬——一個由銀和青玉做成的龍形耳環，那是多羅所戴的耳環。這時，他感到有人用手搭在他的肩膀上，他一顆心開始砰砰地加速跳動起來。他很快站了起來，看到了一張金龍的面具，這才鬆了一口氣。

「噢，感謝老天，原來是你，馬希爾。」他說道。

「快來，我們得走啦。」馬希爾說。

「去哪裡？你還好吧？你的聲音聽起來怪怪的，出了什麼事嗎？」湯姆問。

「先別問，跟我走就是了。」馬希爾說道。

馬希爾緊緊抓住湯姆的臂膀，手指揪著他的手臂，湯姆可以感覺到他的恐懼。

「我們得走啦。」他急著催促道。

「多羅在哪裡？」湯姆帶著驚慌的語氣問道：「我發現她的耳環掉在地上了，你有看到她嗎？她還好嗎？」

馬希爾沒有回答，只是繼續拉著湯姆穿過人群擁擠的中庭，走向拱道。湯姆的步伐開始加快，他知道一定是出事了，而且讓馬希爾心煩意亂。他要有耐性，什麼都不要再問，馬希爾等一下就會跟他說明。

現在他們來到城堡外面，這裡風勢很強，而且寒冷刺骨。湯姆只能看到眼前幾步遠的地方，雖然看不到山谷，但他知道山谷就在附近的腳下。

P. 60

馬希爾貼著城堡的城牆而行，湯姆緊跟在後，這時他聽到了馬廄裡的馬鳴聲和狂風的怒吼聲。最後，馬希爾停下腳步，推開他們面前的一道木門，裡面有人拿著火把，火光映照在湯姆的臉上，讓他一時之間無法看到東西。

「發生什麼事啦？」他喊了出來。

馬希爾把他推進屋內，然後關上厚重的木門。

等到湯姆的眼睛逐漸適應了裡面的光線後，他看到屋子裡有三個人，在門口邊的是一個持槍男子，另外還有兩個人戴著面具，坐在另一頭的角落裡。湯姆馬上就認出了那兩個面具——金龍和姬雅公主。

湯姆轉過身，看著身後戴著面具的男子，只見男子拿掉臉上的金龍面具，然後獰笑道：「無懈可擊的偽裝，對吧？只有一個人有資格戴金龍面具。」

「原來是你，我們在校門口和機場都看過你，你一直在跟蹤馬希爾。」湯姆說。

「你給我閉嘴，乖乖坐下來。」男人說道。

「就照著他說的做，湯姆。」馬希爾的聲音這時從角落那邊傳了過來。

湯姆的目光從馬希爾移到男人身上，看到男人正持槍對著自己，於是只好坐下來。另一人見狀便馬上過來把湯姆的雙手反綁在背後，然後再把他的兩隻腳綁在一起。粗繩子劃傷了他的手腕。

P. 62

「你想從我們這裡得到什麼？」馬希爾問道，語氣中沒有一絲的憤怒或恐懼。

「我想要那顆『光明之星』。」男人開口道。

多羅聽了倒抽一口氣，但馬希爾仍然很冷靜。「全世界只有你和你爸爸兩個人知道它在哪裡。」男人說。

「既然這樣，你就不需要湯姆和多羅了，你放他們走，我會帶你去找光明之星。」馬希爾冷靜地說道。

男人大聲笑了起來，「你當我是笨蛋嗎？你以為我不知道你的氣力有多大嗎？我已經觀察你好幾個月了，你的手腕只要輕輕一動，就可以讓我癱瘓。」

忠誠與友誼

- 一個好的朋友具有什麼樣的特質？
  和同伴一起討論，然後按重要性將
  各種特質列出來。

「他們兩個要留在這裡，我知道如果有這兩個人質在這裡，你就不會逃掉，你不會讓他們的性命陷於危險之中。如果我沒有帶著光明之星回來，我的朋友就會殺了他們，靜靜的兩槍就可以殺掉你的寶貝妹妹和你的死黨。」

P.63

安靜了一會兒之後，馬希爾說道：「我會帶你去拿光明之星，但是現在我警告你，要去的路上很危險，你準備好面對可能的危險了嗎？」

「只要能拿到光明之星，我什麼都不怕。」男人說。

「很好，那我們走吧，我父親一定很快就會派人來尋找我們的。」馬希爾說。

「沒有人會發現你們不見了，因為姬雅公主、雪豹和金龍都還在參加節慶，我那票壞朋友正戴著一模一樣的面具，在那裡冒充你們。皇太子馬希爾，現在我就幫你鬆綁，你要是敢做出一個什麼動作，我朋友就會馬上殺掉公主。」男人說。

馬希爾看著妹妹，一個眼神凶惡、身材矮胖的光頭男子用臂膀勒住多羅的脖子，用另一隻手舉槍對著她的頭。接著馬希爾又轉頭望向湯姆，然後說道：「記住，熟能生巧，請替我照顧好我妹妹。」

「夠啦，別說這些有的沒的。」疤面男子說完後就走到馬希爾旁邊，把綁在他手腳上的繩子割斷，「雙手放在頭上，然後走到門邊，你要是敢怎樣，你妹妹就沒命了。」

這時，那個傢伙把多羅的脖子勒得更緊了，讓她痛得發出尖叫聲。

P.64

馬希爾緩步走向門邊，男子緊跟在後。他把門推開，一陣刺骨的風雪瞬間灌滿了整個房間。馬希爾和男人走進門外的一片漆黑中，然後門又被關上。那個傢伙的槍仍然抵住多羅的頭，他們就這樣坐了半個小時左右，湯姆幾乎連氣也不敢喘一下，這是他生平最漫長的半個小時了。

P.65

最後，用手臂勒住多羅喉嚨的男子終於放開手，他走到屋子的另外一邊坐下來，不過仍然用槍對著他們。

「我們可以說話嗎？」湯姆問。

男子點了點頭。

「什麼是光明之星？」湯姆問道。

「我也不是很清楚，我沒見過，只有

爸爸和馬希爾看過。不過根據傳說，這是世界上最寶貴的一樣東西，價值超過整個亞洲的黃金，有些人說它是一顆巨大的鑽石，但我不清楚。」多羅說。

在此同時，馬希爾和綁匪正在山區一條陡峭的小徑上奮力往上爬。馬希爾對這條小徑很熟，不過現在大雪紛紛，看不到路面。他們的目的地並不遠，不過在這種天況下，至少要走上兩個小時。

這個綁匪對爬山很有經驗，但這趟路讓他爬得很辛苦。

「我要逃脫是很簡單，只是我要怎樣才能救出湯姆和多羅？」馬希爾心想。

地上結了冰，走起來很滑。馬希爾雖然沒有穿上適合爬山的鞋子，但他的腳沒有打滑過。

爬了一個小時之後，他們來到了一處小洞穴，這裡離目的地只剩一半的路程。

P.66

「我們可以在這裡休息幾分鐘。」馬希爾說。

男子也同意了，於是他們坐在洞穴裡冰冷的石頭地上，抱著雙膝，望著洞外那片潔白的雪牆。

「你要光明之星做什麼？」馬希爾問。

「我在北美洲有個做生意的朋友，他會付我一大筆錢買這顆鑽石。」

「我明白了。你是怎麼知道這顆鑽石的事的？」馬希爾笑著說。

「我是記者，寫了很多篇雪豹王國的文章，你可以說我是研究貴國歷史和政治的專家，我朋友知道這一點，於是就

在一天晚上找我跟他吃吃飯。」

綁匪暫停了片刻，回想和傑克‧夏比第一次見面的那天晚上。當時傑克穿了一套破破爛爛的西裝，手肘處還縫著補釘，很難想像他竟是世界級的大富豪。

「他第一次要我幫他拿到這顆鑽石時，我回絕了，因為這些年以來，我對你父親敬重有加，根本不想偷他的東西。不過後來我報社的工作沒了，失業了。因為工作很難找，就愈來愈想走後路發橫財。最後，我打電話給那位朋友，答應替他偷鑽石。」

P.67

馬希爾盯著綁匪的眼睛看了好一會兒，「希望那顆鑽石不會讓你的期待落空。」馬希爾冷淡地說道：「現在我們該走啦。」

馬希爾站起身來，走出山洞，身影沒入雪牆之中。綁匪打了一個冷顫，不過不是因為風雪寒冷刺骨，而是因為迷惑。在這短暫的片刻中，他在男孩的眼裡看到了自己邪惡的行為。他站起身來，想抖掉刺骨的寒氣和心中的疑惑。接著，他跟著馬希爾走出山洞。

到了山洞外面，他只看得到上方石頭上留著的男孩腳印。他緊緊抓住溜滑的石頭，他知道只要踏錯一步路，就可能丟掉性命。他想偷光明之星的決心又回來了，他每走一步，決心就益發強烈。

湯姆和多羅注意到那個傢伙的眼皮快闔上了，他很累，而且不習慣這麼冷的天氣。他們希望他會睡著。

這時多羅打起哈欠，那傢伙也跟著打哈欠，湯姆更是打著哈欠、閉上了眼睛。

不久，多羅也閉起了眼睛。不一會兒，他們聽到了槍枝掉到地上的聲音，那個傢伙已經進入夢鄉了。

「我腰間的袋子裡有一把短劍，」多羅悄聲說道：「短劍雖然很小，但很鋒利，你試試看可不可以拿到。」

P.68

多羅腰間的衣帶上垂掛著一個袋子，裡面是一把小小的金色短劍。湯姆於是設法把身子靠近她，在試了好幾次之後，終於順利地從袋子裡拿出短劍。他把短劍遞給多羅，然後兩個人背對背坐著，多羅接著慢慢把綁住湯姆雙手的繩子割斷。繩子很粗，像是永遠都割不斷似的。那個傢伙現在雖然鼾聲大作，但有可能突然醒來，把短劍奪走。更恐怖的是，他也可能醒來之後向他們開槍。

繩子一割斷，湯姆接著割斷綁住雙腳的繩子，然後小心翼翼地站起來，躡手躡腳地挨近那個傢伙。這時，那個傢伙聽到了湯姆的聲音，便張開了眼睛，不過他看到的並不是湯姆，而是一隻孔武有力的動物，有著白色的大爪子，綠色的眼睛在火光下閃閃發亮，白色的利齒閃閃發光。那是一隻雪豹。

那個傢伙嚇得跳了起來，隨即拔出短劍。

湯姆看著鋒利的刀面對向自己。這時湯姆想起了馬希爾說過的話：「只要你相信自己做得到，你就一定可以做得到。」

湯姆於是一跳躍向對方，瞬間掠住那個傢伙的臂膀。但那個傢伙眼前看到的不是湯姆，而是一隻雪豹，於是掄起短劍向牠刺去。

湯姆急忙往旁邊一閃，但短劍已經刺到了臂膀。湯姆以為會很痛，但並沒有。

P.70

「專注！」他對自己說：「專注！」然後用手指結實地扣住對方的肩膀。

那個傢伙感到雪豹的利爪嵌進了自己的肩膀，而湯姆感到對方的四肢突然變得僵硬起來。湯姆這時很快一個動作把對方一把扭住，使出一記過肩摔，接著傳來對方落地的聲音。

「起來。」他對著那個傢伙吼叫道，看到了對方臉上的恐懼神情。

「快起來。」他吼道，但那個傢伙仍直直地躺在那裡。

「我做到了，我終於做到了。」湯姆說。

湯姆把面具拋向空中，那個傢伙則眼

睜睜看到雪豹躍過他，在屋子裡消失不見了。

「湯姆，我們得趕快走，已經沒有多少時間了。」多羅說。

湯姆於是立刻跑向她，幫她把繩子鬆綁。

「我們快離開這裡。」她說道。

「但是馬希爾呢？他們把他帶到了哪裡？」湯姆問道。

「我不知道，我不知道光明之星放在哪裡，我們去找我爸爸，除了馬希爾，他是唯一知道的人。」多羅說。

湯姆轉開大門的把手，想把門推開，「這門鎖住了。」他說。

「看看鑰匙是不是在那個人身上。」多羅說。

P.71

湯姆很快搜索了那人的衣服，可是沒有找到鑰匙。

「沒有，鑰匙不在這裡，我們該怎麼辦？」湯姆說。

「你退後點。」多羅說道。她凝視著大門，開始努力集中精神。接著她縱身一躍，凌空飛踢大門。厚重的木門晃了一下，但仍緊閉著。多羅再次騰空而起，向大門飛踢過去。這次大門在一個霹啪巨響後向外面飛散，一陣刺骨寒風立刻灌進了屋子裡。

「哇，好冷。」湯姆說。

「快來，湯姆，我們自由了。」多羅說。

「沒錯，我們自由了。」當兩人步出屋外時，湯姆心想：「可是馬希爾還很危險。」

P.72

偌大的雪片在他們四周打轉著，冰冷的寒風刺在他們的臉上。

「我什麼都看不到。」湯姆說。

多羅握住他的手，說道：「貼著城牆走，就可以走到城堡的大門。你記得我們正走在山谷的邊緣，所以一定要很小心地走，只要踏錯一步，我們就會從一千多公尺高的地方摔下去。」

「謝啦，多羅。」湯姆說道：「很高興能知道這種事。」

然後他想起剛剛走來的路。「多羅，當那個傢伙帶我到房間裡時，我一路上都跟在他後面走，不知道距離山谷那麼近。」他說。

「現在先別想這件事。」多羅說完，把他的手握得更緊了，「我們現在只求平安無事。」

多羅和湯姆繼續沿著城堡的城牆緩慢地移動著。

恐懼

- 你害怕什麼？你最大的恐懼是什麼？列出一張表，和同伴分享。
- 在下面這些事情中，你最怕什麼？
  - ☐ 在一個斷掉的滑雪纜車裡進退不得
  - ☐ 晚上獨自一人走過森林
  - ☐ 在一架正遭到劫持的飛機上
  - ☐ 困在地鐵中動彈不得

P.73

城堡的中庭這時已經空無一人，城牆上的燈籠依舊一明一滅地閃爍著，但每個人都進屋子裡躲風雪了，因此當警衛見到多羅和湯姆時很驚。

「我父親在哪裡？」多羅問道：「請馬上帶我們去他那裡。」

「是的，公主。」警衛說。

「有一個人想要綁架我們，不過他已經被我們綁在馬廄隔壁的那個房間裡，現在請你們把他帶到一個比較安全的地方，然後看住他。」

「遵命。」警衛說道。其中一名警衛立刻跑去調來更多的警衛。

所幸國王沒有和賓客在一起，而是獨自一人待在一間像是圖書館的房子裡。

「爸爸！」多羅一見到國王就喊道，然後跑到他面前抱住他。

「怎麼回事？」國王問。

「是馬希爾。」多羅說道，國王的臉色霎時變得一片蒼白。

「他發生了什麼事？」國王問道，聲音依舊保持冷靜。

「他被綁架了。」多羅說。

國王的眼神越過她看著湯姆，「是一直跟蹤他的那個記者幹的嗎？」他問湯姆說。

「是的，就是他沒錯。」湯姆說。

「他有說他為什麼要綁架馬希爾嗎？」國王問。

「有，他想要那顆光明之星，馬希爾正帶著他要去拿光明之星。」多羅說。

P.74

「我明白了。」國王說完便陷入沉思中。

「可是我不知道他們要去哪裡。」多羅說完，便把整件事的原委全告訴父親。

「別擔心，多羅。」父親說道：「我知道他們去了哪裡，我們可以比他們先到達。他們要去月寺，月寺就在這座山的山頂。馬希爾沒有進入城堡，所以我想他已經走上上山的小徑了，在這種天氣下，大概要走上兩個小時。」

「那我們是趕不上他們了。」湯姆說道。

「這座城堡有一條地下通道通到月寺，我們只要沿著這條通道，十分鐘就可以走到了。」國王回答。

就在這時候，一名警衛走了進來，向國王說了一些話。國王下達了若干指示後，警衛便鞠躬告退。

「爸爸，我要跟你一起去。」多羅說。

「我也要去。」湯姆說。

國王沒有異議，他想在馬希爾拿光明之星給記者之前，先一步趕到月寺去。

「我們現在就走。」國王說完便帶領他們進入一道長廊，長廊的盡頭出現一道門，當一行人走到那裡時，一名警衛便把門打開。

接著他們進入狹窄的通道，這時有一排提著燈籠的人出現在他們前面，湯姆看到那些人的腰帶都掛著一支支大劍。

「他們就是節慶上的那些軍人？」他問多羅說。

P.75

「沒錯，見識過他們高超劍術的人，都不敢向他們挑釁。我想那個記者應該知道我們王國的很多事。」多羅說。

狹窄的通道很陡，爬起來很吃力。

他們走到通道底，接著進入一個房間裡，只見房間裡的拱型天花板又高又大，並且漆成深藍色，上面畫滿了銀色和金色的星星，正中間的地方則畫了一個月亮。

房間裡都是身著橘色長袍的僧人，正坐在蓆子上誦經。這時誦經的聲音停了下來，一個身穿橘色長袍的小男孩跑向他們，他的腳步踏在石板上發出陣陣回

聲。他看到國王時，便停下了腳步，並在國王面前行鞠躬禮。

「帶我去光明之星那裡。」國王說。

小男孩又行了一個禮之後，便站起身來。多羅這時走向了父親。

「你不能跟我去，多羅。」國王吩咐道：「你和湯姆找個比較隱密的地方坐下來，等你哥哥來。」

男孩和國王於是走到月寺前方，然後鑽進一道繡工精細的厚重簾幕之後。

「我第一次來這裡。」多羅說完，便抬頭凝視著富麗堂皇的天花板。

P.77

眾僧繼續誦經，軍人則和他們一起坐在蓆子上。湯姆和多羅也走去和僧人坐在一起，多羅跟著一起誦經，湯姆則靜靜地坐著。

這時，月寺的前門突然在一陣嘎嘰作響中打開，兩個白色的人影搖搖晃晃地走了進來，只見僧人們繼續誦經，未加以理會站在門口的兩人。

湯姆見到有個男人手裡拿著槍，並且緊緊抓住馬希爾，用另一隻手臂扣住馬希爾的脖子，他的心不由得揪了起來。接著他又看到那個男人正用槍對著馬希爾的頭。

「把光明之星拿給我。」只見他用冷冰冰的語氣大聲叫道：「不然我就殺了你們尊貴的王子。」

這時有一位僧人從刺繡精美的簾幕後面走了出來，說道：「我會拿光明之星給你，你準備好要看它了嗎？」

「我準備好啦。」男人喊道。

「那麼，請把槍放下。」僧人說道。

男人這時把馬希爾的脖子勒得更緊，讓馬希爾嗆了一下。

「把槍放下，我會拿光明之星給你。」僧人重複說道，語氣很冷靜。

記者這時放開馬希爾，然後彎下腰去，把槍放在地上。

這時國王打開簾幕，只見走出來了一個小男孩。小男孩大約六歲左右，國王牽著他的手，然後兩人一起走向記者。

「這就是光明之星。」國王說道，然後小男孩便往前踏出一步。

P.78

「你騙人。」記者說完便彎腰再度撿起槍。沒有人做出任何動靜。

「光明之星是世界上最寶貴的一樣東西，」國王冷靜地說：「閣下真的認為世界上最寶貴的東西就是鑽石？閣下難道以為世界上最寶貴的東西就是金錢？」

滿足

- 什麼東西對你來說是很重要的？請針對下列各項依其重要性排列出來，並說明原因。
  - ☐ 花時間與朋友共度
  - ☐ 身體健康
  - ☐ 有錢
  - ☐ 功成名就
  - ☐ 在學校裡廣受歡迎
  - ☐ 擁有趕搭流行的衣物
  - ☐ 擁有藝術或音樂上的才華
  - ☐ 擅長運動

記者滿懷驚懼地盯著國王，他現在知道國王不是在撒謊，根本就沒有什麼鑽石。他把槍扔下，兩名軍人隨即跑過去架住他的手臂。

「世界上最寶貴的東西，就是生命。」國王說完便轉過身，帶著小男孩走回簾幕後方。

P.80

多羅跑向馬希爾，緊緊抱住他，「你還好吧？」她問道。

「我很好，只是有點冷。」馬希爾邊說邊向湯姆招了招手，湯姆見狀便跑了過來。

「我想你的厄運是被綁架，那是誰得到了好運？」湯姆說。

「當然是你和多羅啊。」馬希爾說。

「我不懂。」湯姆說。

「我懂，我們運氣很好，才能目睹

光明之星，我們會得到長壽和幸福快樂的。」多羅說。

「嗯，有道理。」湯姆說。他思索了片刻，覺得多羅說得沒有錯。他很幸運，而且他今天也學到了一個寶貴的教訓。

「生命是最不可思議的。」他心想。

假期轉眼就要結束了。湯姆站在房間的陽台上，馬希爾走了過來，站在他身邊。「準備要走了嗎？」馬希爾問道。

「我已經打包好了，但我不確定是不是已經做好了離開這個王國的準備。」湯姆說道：「對了，你父親決定要如何處置那個叫傑克的記者了嗎？」

「你也知道，傑克已經向我爸爸道歉，而且他也很喜歡我們的王國，而且又和我爸爸很合得來。我想他是真的很後悔，我爸爸發自內心原諒了他，不過他當然要為自己的所作所為付出代價，他會在皇宮的監獄裡待上一年。」

P.81

「這很合理，畢竟我們的小命差點葬送在他手裡，我還擔心你父親會放過他呢。」湯姆說。

「我爸不會這樣做的。平常他是不太處罰別人，而且他也很難下得了手。不過，我想他這一次是受到了驚嚇。」

「沒錯，我想我們能順利脫逃是很幸運的。當初我在學校裡打包時，寇尼力還說或許再也看不到我了，差一點被他說中啦。」湯姆說。

「最起碼我們證明了寇尼力又錯了。」馬希爾邊說看著手錶：「我們要趕快走了，不然會趕不上飛機。」

P.82

一個小時後，馬希爾、多羅和湯姆三人就坐在機場的出境大廳裡，再過十五分鐘，湯姆就要離開裡這飛往加德滿都了。

「你在這裡玩得愉快嗎？」多羅問道。

「這可以說是我有史以來最刺激的一次假期了。」湯姆說道。

「難道你不懷念電視？」

「不，我不懷念，我根本沒時間去想電視。不過，我很期待回到英國後可以做一件事。」湯姆說。

「什麼事？」馬希爾問道。

「啃個特大號的漢堡和薯條，而且不加辣椒。」他說完，三個人都哈哈大笑起來。

125

Before Reading

Page 6

1

a) Snow leopards live in Central Asia and the Himalayan Mountains of Bhutan, India, Nepal and Tibet.

b) Adult male snow leopards measure up to 2.10 meters in length (including a tail of up to 1 meter).

c) They need long tails to help them to balance when they leap across the rocky ground.

d) They've got wide noses to help them to breathe because there isn't much oxygen high in the mountains.

e) Their furry feet help them to balance on top of the snow.

f) They eat deer, hares and boars.

g) A snow leopard can jump up to 15 meters.

h) Baby snow leopards weigh half a kilo.

Page 7

3

a) Asia and Europe

b) Thriller

Page 8

5

The first picture is of the grounds of a boarding school in Britain. The second picture is of a monastery in the Himalayas.

6

a) 8   b) 5   c) 6   d) 7

e) 1   f) 3   g) 4   h) 2

Page 9

7

a) monks

b) throne

c) gun

d) arrow

e) cave

f) mask

g) bow

h) temple

After Reading

Page 85

1

Tom: calm, strong.

Mahir: adventurous, kind

Tara: friendly, brave

The King: wise, fair

Page 86

3

a) Tom   b) Mahir   c) Tara

d) Princess Kia   e) Jake

f) The King and Queen

4 a) Tara   b) The King   c) Jake   d) Tom

Page 87

6

a) It is the flash of a camera.

b) Cornelius thinks Tom will be kept prisoner or attacked by a yeti.

c) They see Mount Everest.

d) Tom thinks the man with the scar will hijack the plane.

e) Tara makes a Golden Dragon mask,
   a Snow Leopard mask and a Princess
   Kia mask.
f) Mahir is upset because he hits the
   blue eye of the black dragon.
g) Jake kidnaps Tom, Tara and Mahir
   because he wants to steal the
   Shining Star.
h) Jake thinks the Shining Star is a
   diamond.
i) Tom and Tara are lucky because they
   will be rewarded with long life and
   happiness.
j) Tom will eat a whopper hamburger
   and French fries, without chili
   peppers.

7
a) The Shining Star
b) The snow leopard
c) The King and Queen
d) The monkey
e) The horse
f) The bird
g) The snow
h) The blue sky

Page 89
8
a) 1 b) 3 c) 2 d) 3
e) 1 f) 1 g) 2 h) 1

Page 90
10 a) 5 b) 4 c) 2 d) 3 e) 1

11
1) yet/already; yet
2) yet/already; just/already
3) yet/already; just/already
4) just

Page 91
12
a) don't have to
b) has to
c) have to
d) have to

Page 92
13
a) lets
b) lets
c) make
d) makes
e) makes

14
a) is eaten
b) is worn
c) were greeted
d) were made
e) was rescued
f) were kidnapped
g) was taken
h) was punished

Project Work

Page 94
1
1. Himalayan 2. cars 3. horses
4. bicycles 5. spicy 6. chili peppers
7. vegetarians 8. yak 9. archery
10. competition 11. women
12. have to 13. 5,000

Page 95
4
a) 1 b) 2 c) 3 d) 1 e) 3

國家圖書館出版品預行編目資料

雪豹王國 / Elspeth Rawstron著；李璞良 譯. —初
版. —[臺北市]：寂天文化, 2012.9　面；公分.

中英對照

ISBN 978-986-318-037-1 (25K平裝附光碟片)

1.英語　2.讀本

805.18　　　　　　　　　　101017328

作者 _ Elspeth Rawstron

譯者 _ 李璞良

校對 _ 陳慧莉

封面設計 _ 蔡怡柔

主編 _ 黃鈺云

製程管理 _ 蔡智堯

出版者 _ 寂天文化事業股份有限公司

電話 _ +886-2-2365-9739

傳真 _ +886-2-2365-9835

網址 _ www.icosmos.com.tw

讀者服務 _ onlineservice@icosmos.com.tw

出版日期 _ 2012年9月 初版一刷（250101）

郵撥帳號 _ 1998620-0 寂天文化事業股份有限公司

訂購金額600 （含）元以上郵資免費

訂購金額600元以下者，請外加郵資60元

若有破損，請寄回更換

〔限台灣銷售〕